Romance Unbound Publishing
Presents

Submission in Paradise

Claire Thompson

Edited by
Donna Fisk
Jae Ashley

Cover Art by Kelly Shorten
Fine Line Edit by Kevin Gherlone

Print ISBN 9781494801243
Copyright 2014 Claire Thompson
All rights reserved

Chapter 1

Shea flicked between screens on her computer as she executed a few rapid fire calculations. "That's right, Ben," she said into the phone. "Now that I've had a chance to really delve into your financials, I recommend we raise capital through equity sales rather than debt." She became aware of Jackie standing by her desk with some kind of brochure in her hand. The phone wedged under her chin, Shea waved a hand to indicate Jackie should have a seat.

Jackie, Shea's immediate boss and closest friend, began drumming her perfectly manicured nails on the edge of Shea's desktop with an impatient clicking tattoo. "I really don't think that's a concern," Shea continued into the phone, while mouthing, "Just a sec'," to Jackie. "Their clean capital structure and industry niche make them an ideal candidate. This deal is a win-win." Shea offered a smile and eye roll toward Jackie as her latest client, a skittish CEO she was guiding through a merger, rambled on. Finally able to extricate herself, Shea made her goodbyes and promised to send her finalized proposal by the end of the day.

Shea turned her attention to Jackie. "What's up?"

Jackie pushed the glossy brochure across the desk. Shea reached for it, lifting her eyebrows as she read the cover. *Paradise Islands – Passion Individually*

Tailored for the Woman with Everything but Time. An impossibly gorgeous male model was lying half-naked on a chaise lounge against a backdrop of white sand and an azure sea.

"What's this? A new takeover target?"

"No," Jackie replied briskly. "It's where you're going to be spending a week off."

Shea gave a small laugh as she pushed the brochure back toward Jackie. "Cute, but I don't have time for a vacation. I have two mergers to complete and that venture capital deal in the works."

Jackie's face assumed her I-am-queen-you-will-do-as-I-say expression that had brought more than a few high-powered financial bigwigs to heel. "Here's a newsflash for you, sweetie. The world will continue to revolve and Sutton Investments to function, even if Shea Devon takes some time off for the first time in three years."

Shea opened her mouth to protest but Jackie didn't give her a chance. "Not a word, missy. Look at you. Did you even go home last night?"

Shea was unable to stop her guilty glance toward the wardrobe in the corner of her office where she kept spare suits when pulling an all-nighter. Jackie, who rarely missed a trick, chortled, "Aha! Guilty as charged." Her smile slid away as she leaned forward, her eyes filled with concern. "Shea, sweetie, listen to me. You know how valued you are here, but I think you've forgotten there's more to life than work. When was the last time you even went out on a date?"

"I don't have time—"

"Exactly my point," Jackie interrupted. "You're a kickass investment banker who's made a bundle for this firm, but there's more to life than crunching numbers and structuring mergers. Do you want to end up like Howard Williams? I don't think Howard even noticed when his wife divorced him—he was too busy closing a deal." Jackie waved a hand toward the large window that looked out over Houston's downtown skyline. "There's a whole world out there passing you by."

With uncharacteristic gentleness, Jackie pushed the brochure back in Shea's direction. "Just have a look at it, okay? Try to keep an open mind. Who can say no to a week of pampering and pleasure with zero strings attached? That's why I bought it for you. It was tailor-made for a busy executive like you."

"Wait, what?" Shea was taken aback. "You already bought it?"

Jackie nodded firmly. "Yep. It's bought and paid for. I know the owner and I know a couple of women who have availed themselves of the, uh, talent that works there. The company has a one-hundred percent satisfaction rate." She reached across the desk and patted the brochure. "Consider it an early bonus. If you decide this Paradise Islands thing isn't for you, don't worry, I can get most of the money back. But you *will* take a vacation, and soon. It's either that, or you're fired."

"Ha, ha. Very funny." Shea laughed, expecting Jackie to join in. When she didn't, Shea saw the serious expression on Jackie's face. "Wait a minute. You're not serious?" Shea sputtered indignantly.

"To be perfectly blunt, you're burning out, Shea. You have no life outside of this place. It isn't healthy. You're not going to be of much use to anybody if you end up keeling over dead of a heart attack at the age of thirty-two. You *need* some time off. Refill the coffers, get some rest and relaxation." Jackie grinned. "Why not spend that week getting wined, dined and pampered by someone like that hunk there, eh?"

Shea shook her head, aware Jackie wouldn't leave her alone until she at least looked at the darn thing. She flipped open the brochure, both irritated and touched by Jackie's obvious concern for her welfare. There were more pictures of beautiful beach locales and gorgeous men, along with captions including: *Choose your fantasy – wine, roses and candlelight; a BDSM island fantasy with the Master of your dreams; get swept off your feet by the shy but passionate boy next door. All vacation packets are provided in the idyllic setting of a private island located in the Caribbean, less than an hour's plane ride from Florida. We tailor your week of intimate romance precisely to your desires. We will select your ideal* man, based on information you provide. *All you need to do is show up and surrender to a week of pure indulgence."*

Shea laughed as she looked up at Jackie. "Is this for real?"

Jackie nodded emphatically. "It sure is. It's very exclusive—by invitation only. If I wasn't married to Jerry, you can bet I'd be signing up in a heartbeat."

"It must cost a fortune," Shea mused.

"That's not your concern," Jackie snapped, though she was grinning. "Anyway, you've earned it and then some. Think about it, Shea. A week of romance on a private Caribbean island with a guy you never have to see again—what could be better?"

"You're talking about hiring some kind of, what, male prostitute?" Shea protested, though she was intrigued.

"Don't be so gauche," Jackie retorted. "From what I understand, they're all highly trained and very professional. They know how to give a woman a week she'll never forget. As to the sex part" —Jackie shrugged, though her smile was wicked—"that part is up to you. I bought you the deluxe package, the very top of the line. That means you get whatever you want—that's *whatever* you want, Shea. I have it on good authority that all the men who work there are clean, gorgeous and highly skilled in the, uh, sexual arts. How far you choose to go is, apparently, entirely up to you."

Shea offered a few more excuses and refusals, but in the end, as she'd known would happen, Jackie wore her down. Shea made the appointment and two days later drove to the posh River Oaks location where she spent an hour filling out a detailed questionnaire about her dream fantasy and perusing the photographs of sexy guys on staff ready to "make her dreams come true." She had been surprised, though she supposed she shouldn't have been, by the smorgasbord of sexual choices and predilections to choose from. She went for what was called the traditional package—a week of relaxation on the beach, snorkeling, massages and romance by candlelight.

It all happened so fast, and within a few days, Shea received an email confirmation of her flight information. In a way she was glad that the "dream packet" she had chosen didn't allow for the selection of a particular guy. It would be kind of fun to be surprised, and if didn't work out, she wouldn't spend time second-guessing her choice.

Before she knew it, Shea was packing for a week of hedonistic pleasure on a private island with a man she'd never met. "Worse comes to worst," she told herself as she glanced down at her pale, indoor office skin, "I'll work on my tan."

~*~

Brittany grinned down at the text from Rob. Maybe tonight was the night. She'd move from flirtation and teasing to the next step, and let him take her home from the dance club. She picked up her phone, thumbs poised to reply when a strident voice nearly shocked her out of her wits.

Dropping the phone, Brittney pushed some files over it as she looked up to find Sylvia Henley, owner of Paradise Islands, and Brittany's new boss, staring accusatorially down at her.

"I'm sorry, what?" Brittany said, flustered.

"I said," Sylvia repeated in a crisp tone, "What've we got for the meeting this week? Are the files ready?" Maybe she hadn't witnessed the texting. Phew.

Brittany lifted her chin and flashed a dimpled smile, reminding herself she was way younger and way better looking than her boss. "We have three new packets and they're all ready and typed. There were four, but one canceled at the last minute."

Sylvia nodded. "Make sure to shred the canceled packet. We pride ourselves on our discretion. Make two additional copies of each of the other packets and bring them to the boardroom for my three o'clock. Make a fresh pot of coffee and put out those croissants I brought in this morning. Your attendance won't be necessary."

"Yes, ma'am," Brittany replied to the woman's retreating back as she clicked away on her Prada heels. Fine with her—she would be able to text without anyone breathing down her neck.

Brittany waited until Sylvia had disappeared into her office before pushing the folders aside to see what Rob had texted. *Babe, I can't get you out of my head. Let's make tonight magical.* Brittany shivered with excited anticipation but then glanced at the clock. Shit. It was nearly three already.

She picked up the files, along with her phone, which was buzzing again with another text from the sexy Rob. As she headed toward the shredder at the end of the hall, she tucked the folders under her arm so she could read Rob's text.

Harry Stern chose that moment to come out of the men's bathroom just as Brittany was passing by. Harry, who was hot for an older guy, wasn't watching where he was going, and his shoulder slammed into Brittany before she could get out of the way. The folders went flying, though she managed to keep hold of her phone, thank goodness.

"Oh, sorry," Harry said with a distracted air. "I didn't see you there." Brittany squatted and reached for the scattered papers, annoyed when Harry made no effort to assist. "Heading to the meeting," he said by way of apology, she supposed.

Stressed, Brittany grabbed at the papers. Two of the questionnaires had fallen out of their respective folders, and Brittany wasn't sure which one she was supposed to shred. Those rich bitches with money to burn had a lot of nerve making her type up pages and pages of their pathetic sexual fantasies.

She glanced down the hall to see if anyone was watching her. Damn it, she didn't have time for this! She still had to make the coffee. How was she supposed to keep track of all this crap, anyway? She should have kept the job at the mall. With an exasperated shrug, she picked up one of the questionnaires and shoved it into a folder. If there was a problem, let someone else sort it out. It wasn't her fault.

Putting the whole mess firmly out of her mind, Brittney continued down the hall to the shredder. She slid the pages of what she hoped was the canceled questionnaire through the noisy machine, turning her mind to what outfit she would wear that night, and more importantly, what sexy underclothes she would wear beneath it.

~*~

"Liam Jordan."

"Liam. Glad I caught you. I have a job for you."

Liam swiveled in his chair so he could face the large picture window behind his desk. "Hey, Sylvia. I'm fine, thanks. And you?"

"Oh, you Brits with your need for ceremony. Okay, okay. How are you, Liam?" Without giving him a chance to respond, she continued, "Sorry, but

I've got a crisis on my hands. Jack Morris was scheduled to take a *BDSM Dream Island* client scheduled for the end of the week, and he just called me from the emergency room. He's been in a car accident."

"Is he okay?" Liam liked Jack and had worked extensively with him to get him up to speed as the primary Dom-in-residence at Sylvia's company before Liam left to pursue his own aims.

"Yeah, but he broke his damn leg and now I've got to come up with a replacement. If it were one of the vanilla packages, you know I could handle it, no problem. But you're the only other person I know who can deal with the full BDSM fantasy packet. This woman wants the whole shebang. She's looking for a Master, with a capital M. I really need your help. The company's stellar reputation is at stake."

Liam shook his head, smiling ruefully at his cell phone. "Sylvia, I don't work for you anymore, remember? I have my own business to run and—"

"Her name is Shea Devon," Sylvia continued, as if Liam hadn't spoken. "Age thirty-two, single, never married, clean bill of health and ready to rumble. She claims to be a bad girl, you know, the kind who needs to be controlled."

"Sylvia, I—"

"Help me out here just this once, and I'll owe you big time. Listen, I'll throw you eighty percent of the fee. I'll just keep enough for expenses. This packet was purchased by a high-powered investment banker friend of mine, well connected in the Houston financial community. My reputation is at stake here. Please, Liam, I'm desperate," Sylvia entreated. "It's just this once. I'm begging you."

Since Liam's investments had panned out so well, he no longer needed to work for others. Sylvia had been mostly understanding when he had told her he was striking out to start up his own training business for serious men and women with a real commitment to the lifestyle. But she was like a bulldog with a bone when she wanted something, and could be very persistent. Liam chuckled.

"I know that laugh," Sylvia snapped. "Don't give me that laugh. At least look at her photo before you dismiss this out of hand. Hold on. I'm sending it now."

Liam's phone vibrated. He clicked open the text message with a head shot that quite literally took his breath away. The woman's blue-gray eyes seemed to stare right into his soul from the screen. She had dark, glossy hair, high cheekbones and a lush mouth that put him in mind of bruised strawberries. A second message came through with a second photo, this one a full body shot. Dressed in a knit top and jeans, it was clear the woman had curves in all the right places. Liam instantly envisioned her naked, rope around her wrists and ankles, her body taut and trembling in anticipation.

"Liam? Did you get the pics? Will you do it? Just this once?"

"I'd have to do some juggling to clear my schedule," Liam found himself saying. "What day did you need me?"

"This coming Sunday. It's just a one week commitment. Oh, thank you, thank you, thank you! I'll scan and email her file as soon as we hang up. You're the best." Sylvia clicked off before Liam could protest.

How the hell had that just happened?

Liam looked again at the picture of Shea Devon's face, his lips suddenly burning at the thought of kissing that mouth. It was just for a week. He had a few appointments, but he could reschedule those.

A moment later his email pinged. Liam swiveled back to his computer and opened the mail from Sylvia, curious to see Shea's questionnaire. He frowned as he read the words.

Shea had written that she wanted to be kept in chains and forced to stay in a cage, her every move controlled by a stern taskmaster. She wanted to be "trained in the art of erotic submission," and had noted she was "a brat who needs to be reminded of my place. I like a good fight and I need a strong man who won't take any of my sass. I need a good, hard spanking from a man willing and able to keep me in line. I'm seriously into erotic pain and I crave the whip, the crop, the cane and the paddle. My fantasy is to play the innocent—a poor young girl with no idea what she's getting into. I like to pretend to resist, but in the end, I am longing to surrender." Under the section called "hard limits" the woman had written: NONE. Her safeword was "black-and-blue".

Liam was disappointed. It was hard to reconcile the words on the computer screen with the grave young woman staring at him from his phone. He had never been a fan of the "brat" genre of BDSM play, which smacked too much of a game for his taste, and in his opinion diminished the intensity of a true D/s experience.

He shrugged. *Lighten up, Jordan*. He was doing a favor for Sylvia, nothing more. Being paid handsomely to spend a luxurious week on a private Caribbean island with a gorgeous woman, however insincere she might be, wasn't the worst fate in the world. And who knew, maybe there was more to the beautiful Shea Devon than her playful, if rather superficial, questionnaire indicated. If so, Liam Jordan was the man to find out.

Chapter 2

The warm, salt-scented wind blew Shea's hair back as the speed boat bounced lightly over water that looked like turquoise glass. It was hard to believe she'd spent the morning fighting the abysmal Houston traffic and then juggling her way through the crowded airport, only to be squashed into a commuter plane to Miami with seats that seemed to have been designed for anorexic children. The next leg of her journey had been much more satisfactory — a private plane with two other passengers, both women on their way to their own private fantasy island.

Her companions appeared to be in their late forties or early fifties, and seemed to know each other. They asked her if she'd ever done this before, to which she admitted she had not. Each gave a knowing laugh and assured her she was in for the week of a lifetime. Despite misgivings about what the hell she was getting herself into, Shea couldn't help the flutter of nervous excitement in her gut at the thought of a week with a strange man whose sole purpose was to pamper and indulge her.

The women had chatted away nonstop to one another about ex-spouses, children, their lives in general and their *sexcation* fantasy packets, as they called them. Their raucous laughter as they debated the merits of their chosen fantasy got louder with each champagne cocktail they imbibed. Shea stuck to sparkling water, glad she'd brought her Kindle.

The plane landed at Aruba, and a small boat was waiting to take them on to their respective paradise island vacations. The other women had been deposited first, each on a tiny speck of an island not much bigger than a football field, so it seemed to Shea. In each case a very handsome guy was there on the dock to help each tittering woman from the boat. Both guys seemed almost young enough to be the women's sons, but neither woman seemed in the least perturbed by this.

Now it was Shea's turn. The pilot, a man named Scott with a leathery tan beneath a shock of thick gray hair, cut the engine and coasted toward a small dock. Shea's pulse quickened as she saw a tall figure with broad shoulders and light brown hair streaked with gold that caught the sunlight. He was wearing a white T-shirt and dark blue shorts that revealed muscular legs covered in golden down. Her nipples were poking visibly against the sheer fabric of her sundress, but she told herself it was because of the cold sea spray kicked up by the boat.

As they angled to the side of the dock, the man lifted a hand in greeting and smiled, revealing white teeth against tan skin. Though his face was partially obscured by sunglasses, she could see he had a hawkish nose and a strong jaw, both of which she approved. As they got closer, she guessed her mystery date to be in his early to mid thirties. She breathed a sigh of relief at this—she really didn't want to spend a week with a twentysomething pretty boy, no matter how much he pampered her.

Scott jumped effortlessly to the dock and reached for a rope to secure the boat. As he bent down to retrieve Shea's suitcase, the handsome man on the dock extended his hand, and Shea, though she could have easily stepped out of the boat without assistance, accepted it. His hands were large and strong, his grip firm as he helped her onto the dock.

"Everything good here?" Scott asked.

The man glanced at Shea, and she nodded, not knowing what else to do. She'd come this far, hadn't she? With a nod of his own, the man turned back to Scott. "Good to go, Scott. Thanks for everything and have a safe trip back to the mainland." His voice was deep and rich, with a luscious hint of a British accent. Was that a put-on, or was this guy actually from England? Either way, Shea couldn't deny she loved it.

Scott started the boat's engine and sped away over the water, his boat leaving a V of crystalline waves in its wake. Shea watched the boat as it headed away from them, a part of her wanting to call out for the pilot to return and take her with him. Her heart was beating absurdly fast and she could scarcely believe this was actually happening. The whole thing still seemed so surreal.

Finally, not knowing what else to do, Shea turned to the man standing beside her, who turned to her at the same time. "Welcome to paradise," he said as he removed his sunglasses. Though she would have expected blue eyes with his blond-streaked hair and coloring, his eyes were in fact brown, a deep liquid brown.

"My name is Liam," he said in that gorgeous accent. "Liam Jordan." He extended his hand and Shea automatically extended her own.

"Shea Devon," she replied, though she realized belatedly that he had to know that. Instead of the firm shake she was used to in the business world, Liam lifted her fingers to his lips. His kiss was brief, a warm brush against her skin that made Shea draw in her breath. He let her hand go and reached toward her, his fingers tracing lightly over her throat.

Startled, Shea pulled back, feeling a warmth flood her cheeks that had nothing to do with the sun. Liam was gazing at her with a dark, intense look that made her insides flutter uncomfortably. She looked away, lifting a hand to her throat in confusion.

Liam touched her shoulder. "Shea, let me take you to see our accommodations. The sun will be setting soon, and so our adventure begins." He flashed a brilliant smile at Shea. Their adventure—

yes, of course. He was just playing a part. She would play hers too.

"That sounds good," Shea agreed, offering him what she hoped was an assured smile. Liam lifted her suitcase and they walked along the thin strip of powdery white sand through a row of palm trees. As they came out on the other side, she saw a large bungalow with a thatched roof and whitewashed adobe walls set on sturdy stilts several feet off the ground. It was nestled in a riot of brightly colored blossoms.

"Wow," she exclaimed as she walked along the path to the door. "This looks like the set of a movie or something."

They walked up the steps to the front door. "Let me show you inside," Liam said in his rich, sexy voice. He pushed the door open and gestured Shea inside. If the outside of the bungalow had looked like a movie set, the inside looked like something out of *Architectural Digest* magazine. There was a sense of open airiness in the large room, with its white walls, white furniture, huge picture windows and high ceilings. Plush white area rugs were scattered over floors of dark, shiny hardwood.

"Let's put your case in here and then we can have something to eat. I imagine you must be hungry after a full day of travel." Though Shea hadn't been focused on the idea of food, his remark woke her tummy, which growled in peeved agreement.

She followed her host, or whatever the heck he was, into a large bedroom. Against one wall stood a four-poster bed with white linens and a sheer white voile draped prettily between the posts. One entire wall of the room was comprised of huge windows that looked out at the ocean lapping against the other side of the tiny island.

Outside the windows, which Shea now saw included French doors set in their center, was a veranda shaded with thatch, beneath which sat two lounge chairs facing the ocean, a small table between them.

"If you'd like to freshen up," Liam said with wave toward what must be the bathroom, "I'll get dinner going. We'll have a simple supper tonight, if that's okay. I find a light meal after travel is best."

"That sounds great," Shea agreed, her full bladder urging her toward the spacious blue and white tiled bathroom.

"Perfect. The kitchen's just through the living room. I'll see you there." Liam smiled, his eyes crinkling at the corners, and something tugged hard inside Shea. While she had known the actor who would be "servicing" her for the week would be good looking, she hadn't expected the strong visceral reaction she was experiencing in his presence. Jackie was right—she'd been working with her nose to the grindstone for far too long. She could barely remember the last time she'd gone on a date with a guy, much less spent an entire week getting to know him.

Not that she'd actually be getting to know him, she told her image in the mirror as she washed her hands and splashed water on her face. Not the *real* Liam Jordan, if that was even his name. He was performing a role, executing a part, and really, so was she. The entire construct was artificial by its very nature.

And that's all to the good, Shea reminded herself. She had no time for relationships, not at this point in her career, and especially not with an actor willing to provide his sexual services to any woman with a bank account fat enough to pay for it.

She considered changing out of her sundress into a tank top and shorts, but decided she was too hungry for that. She made her way past a closed door she presumed must be the second bedroom, and back through the airy living room into the kitchen. She was greeted by white wooden cabinets and black granite countertops.

Liam showed her to a small table set in a nook in the corner of the kitchen beneath a window overlooking a thicket of tropical foliage that gleamed darkly beneath a setting sun. On the table was a cold spread of chicken salad, bread and cheese, and fresh fruit. In addition to glasses of ice water stood a chilled bottle of white wine, two wineglasses at the ready beside it.

Dinner passed quite pleasantly and Shea relaxed. The food was delicious, the white wine a perfect complement. After a couple of glasses, Shea ended up sharing more than she'd planned about her work and her life as Liam teased information from her with remarkable grace. He was attentive without being obtrusive, and seemed genuinely fascinated with everything she had to say. Even though she tried to remind herself he was being paid to be interested, she opened up, confiding more about the stress of her job than she usually admitted to anyone, as well her loneliness since she'd moved to Houston to make her mark in the financial community.

After dinner, Liam made some espresso coffee that he served in small cups. Shea bit into a delicious piece of shortbread and sipped at the strong coffee, wondering suddenly where the two of them would sleep. Would Liam stay in the other bedroom or would they be expected to tumble into bed right off the bat?

Unwilling to bring up the issue yet, instead she said, "I've been monopolizing this conversation. Tell me about you." She wanted to ask how he'd gotten into this particular line of business as a professional gigolo, but decided that would ruin the mood.

"You're from England, right? What brought you to the States?"

"My mother was born in Texas. My parents got divorced and my mother and I moved back here when I was seventeen. I could have stayed in London, but I wanted the adventure of something totally new. I went to Rice University and took my degree in physics. I worked as an associate professor at Rice for a few years, but finally had to admit that academia wasn't really my thing. Too much politics for my taste. And I found I had other, uh, talents."

I bet you did, Shea thought, but didn't voice. They chatted amiably about their respective childhoods and other topics for a while, and Shea began to wish this was a real date with a real guy. Acting or not, Liam struck her as someone she would like to know better, even if he was just working a paid gig.

After the meal, they cleared the table together. Shea watched as Liam rinsed the dishes and put away the food, surreptitiously admiring the long lines of his legs and the curve of his firm ass as he moved around the kitchen.

He brought their wineglasses to the counter where Shea stood and filled them with the last of the bottle. He raised his glass and Shea raised hers as well, touching the rim to his. "To a beautiful woman who understands the power of erotic submission."

"I'm sorry, what?"

Liam's lips curved into a slow, sensuous smile. "Ah yes," he said softly, "the innocent. I had nearly forgotten."

Shea furrowed her brow, wondering what the hell Liam was talking about. He took the wineglass from her hand and set it on the counter. Facing her, he leaned forward. He smelled good, like the ocean mingled with the scent of Bay Rum cologne.

This is it! He's going to kiss me.

Shea felt as giddy as any teenager on their first date. Her lips actually tingled with anticipation. Liam dipped his head, his lips lightly brushing hers. Shea closed her eyes and parted her lips, eager to feel the touch of his tongue against hers.

She was flustered when he pulled away, and she opened her eyes and looked up at him. She was startled by the intensity of his gaze, and her heart executed a loop-de-loop in her chest as he began to speak.

"All your life," Liam said softly in his deep, rich voice, "you've been waiting for the right man to claim you."

The words sent a thrill through Shea's loins, though she forced a laugh at the arcane language. "Claim me, huh? And here I had no idea."

Liam didn't smile back. His dark eyes glittered. "You need a strong man, one who can take you in hand. One who understands your deep-seated need to submit. Your longing to surrender."

"What the hell?" Shea blurted, confused. She was startled into silence when Liam placed two fingers against her lips.

"Shh," he said, his mouth close to her ear. "From this moment forward you belong to me. Your submission begins now, slave girl."

~*~

To Liam's surprise, Shea ducked beneath his arm and whirled to face him, her hands on her hips. "Slave girl?" she demanded. "What the hell? This is your idea of romance?"

Liam lifted his eyebrows. No trained slave girl would have dared to speak to him like that, but then, Shea was hardly trained, that much was obvious. He regarded her as he thought through his next move. She looked impossibly lovely standing there in her flimsy sundress, her luminous eyes sparking with what appeared to be genuine indignation. Liam had the sudden nearly overpowering desire to yank the spaghetti straps from her shoulders and bare her breasts. He ached to twist her nipples until she gasped her apology for her impertinence.

Of course, he understood she was just playing a role, the one she'd outlined in her questionnaire, the contents of which he'd nearly managed to put out of his mind during their very pleasant dinner. He was a hired hand, he reminded himself. It was time he did his job.

My fantasy is to play the innocent — a poor young girl with no idea what she's getting into. I like to pretend to resist, but in the end I am longing to surrender. She had written that she was seriously into erotic pain, so obviously she was no newcomer to the scene. She wanted to be challenged and ultimately dominated by someone willing to "force" her into line. While the scenario wasn't really his cup of tea, who was he to question or judge her? He would play his part, and play it well. She would get her money's worth, all right.

Maybe he'd overplayed the first hand in their prearranged game by stating she was his slave girl. It appeared she wanted to take it slower — to continue to pretend she had no idea what was going to happen. He'd had to bite his tongue over dinner to keep the conversation purely vanilla, but clearly she wanted to continue that particular charade a little longer. Fine — he would go along. Yet it wouldn't do to backtrack. It might throw her out of the fantasy.

"There are many kinds of romance, Shea. For some it's the lingering touch of a man's lips on yours, or the shiver of anticipation when he draws his hand along your inner thigh. For others, it's the smell of leather and sweat, the snug embrace of rope, the sudden flick of the cane against tender flesh."

Her mouth had parted softly as he spoke and a flush was creeping up her throat. He reached for her hand. "Come with me. I have something to show you." He was pleased when she let him take her hand. He led her into the second bedroom of the bungalow, which he had personally and lovingly equipped back when he used to work for Paradise Islands.

"Oh my god," Shea said softly. "Do all the vacation islands have this kind of setup? This is wild." She stared wide-eyed around the room as if she'd never seen a BDSM dungeon in her life. Ah yes, the innocent. The girl was an excellent actress, he'd give her that.

He could play that game for as long as she liked. It was her fantasy week, after all. "For the true sexual masochist," he offered, "just the sight of an erotic torture chamber is enough to get the juices flowing. Her imagination places her immediately at the center of each potential scenario."

He led her first to the floor stocks, a free-standing unit of polished wood. "The stocks are just the thing for naughty girls in need of a time-out. A couple of hours in there and you'll think twice before sassing your Master." He regarded her as she took it in. She was still managing that deer-caught-in-the-headlights look quite well. Had she practiced it in the mirror, he wondered sardonically.

He showed her to the spanking bench. "I like this bench because it's adjustable and can be used in a variety of positions. And see," he pointed, "it has attachment rings on each leg with I bolts across the sides, so once I place you on the bench, you aren't going anywhere. Don't worry, though, it's got a nice soft pad across the top to keep you comfortable while I flog you."

"F-flog me?"

Her portrayal of horrified innocence was so realistic Liam almost believed it. He offered an appreciative snort in response and led her to the next area. "This is one of my favorite pieces. It's called a pivot table, and it's a combination of both your traditional medical exam table and a bondage chair. It's really quite ingenious." He pointed to the red leather apparatus, unable to keep the pride from his voice. "See here, the leg and armrests can be spread for ease of access and the padded backrest can be angled so the subject can lie flat or sit erect or anything in between."

Shea had nothing to say to this, Liam was amused to note. He continued the tour. He pointed to the sturdy wooden ladder hanging from chains at its four corners. "Notice how it's chained to the ceiling beam so I can raise and lower it. Imagine being stripped naked and suspended from the rack, your toes barely touching the ground, completely at my mercy."

He glanced at his client to gauge her reaction. Shea was nervously biting her lip. She was good, all right. If she hadn't told him over dinner she was an investment banker, he would have bet money she was a professional actor.

Finally he brought Shea to the St. Andrew's Cross, a staple of any well-equipped dungeon. Time to take her measure in a more concrete way. When she turned to face him, he couldn't help but see the perk of erect nipples straining against the silky fabric of her dress. His cock nudged hard in his shorts. He couldn't remember the last time he'd been so instantly and completely attracted to someone.

Down boy. Time for seduction later. First set the scene.

"Step up to the cross so you can see what's it like to be tethered." *As if you don't know.* He guided Shea onto the small platform at the base of the cross, glad that for the moment at least she had dropped the naive bit. "Lift your arms to either side of the X," he instructed. "That's it. Place your wrists in the cuffs, just so. Feel the extension of your muscles as you stretch upward, and the release of tension when the restraints are locked into place."

He moved close behind her, his cock stiffening into full erection as his groin brushed her ass. When he closed the cuffs around her slender wrists he felt a shiver move through her body. He wanted to kiss her, but that wouldn't do. He had a role to play.

He stepped back. "Spread your legs so I can cuff your ankles."

Shea twisted her head around. "This is wild," she said, her voice breathless. "Do people really do this stuff? I mean, for real?"

She certainly was laying it on thick. Liam offered an ironic smile. "They really do. As if you didn't know, sub girl," he couldn't resist adding.

Shea struggled ineffectually in the wrist cuffs. "Ha ha. Let me out of this thing now." There was a convincing whisper of panic in her tone.

Liam lifted his eyebrows, aware he was expected to refuse. Not intending to disappoint, he offered an evil grin. "Let you out? Whatever for? Don't you want to feel the cut of the cane, the sting of the whip, the smack of the paddle?"

Ignoring her snort of feigned protest, he crouched behind her and pushed her legs apart. With a few deft motions, he the secured the nylon cuffs around her ankles and pressed them closed with the Velcro strips. He had modified the original cross, which had come with stiff leather cuffs that had to be buckled into place. He'd found, especially after intense sessions, that it was a good idea to get his subject out of the cuffs quickly with a minimum of fumbling.

"Hey!" Shea cried, "What the hell are you doing? I said let me out of this thing, this instant!"

Liam stood and pressed his body against hers. "Shh," he murmured against her soft hair. She smelled good and he inhaled deeply. Recalling her claim that she liked to pretend to resist, but in the end was longing to surrender, he said, "You're not exactly in a position to argue, little girl. You'll take what I give you and then you'll thank me for it."

He could feel the tremble in her limbs. She was really getting into this. He must be doing what she wanted. He probably should have made her strip first, but they had a whole week, after all. Better to ramp up the anticipation, both hers and, he realized, his own.

"Damn it!" Shea shouted, startling Liam with the vehemence in her tone as she jerked hard against the cuffs. "I said let me out of this thing. What's wrong with you?"

"With me? I was just going to ask you the same question." Liam brought his hand down hard on her ass, again wishing she was naked.

"Ow!" Shea cried, outrage ripe in her voice. "How *dare* you?"

"Like this. This is how I dare." Liam bent and pulled open Shea's ankle cuffs. He stood and reached for her wrist cuffs, yanking these free as well. When Shea whirled around to face him, he lowered his head and ducked toward her with open arms. Catching her by the waist, he lifted her up over his shoulder before she had a chance to register what he was doing.

Though a part of him knew this was all a game, he was nearly carried away with the scene, eager to get this naughty girl stripped so he could give her the punishment she so richly deserved. He carried her kicking and screaming to the daybed set against the back wall and threw her without ceremony facedown onto the mattress.

A line from her profile played in his head: *I need a good, hard spanking from a man willing and able to keep me in line.* "You know what you need?" he said as he puffed to catch his breath. "You need a good, hard spanking."

"Like hell I do," Shea grunted, struggling beneath his grip. Keeping one hand firmly on the back of her neck, he pulled at the flimsy sundress and yanked it down her lithe form. While she gasped and struggled, he pulled her pretty pink panties down her long, shapely legs.

Liam was surprised at the creamy smoothness of her ass and thighs. For someone "seriously into erotic pain" who claimed to "crave the whip, the crop, the cane and the paddle", her skin was curiously mark-free. There wasn't even a hint of old welts or fading bruises that marked a serious player in the BDSM scene.

Shea was struggling in his grip, her sexy, breathless cries of protest utterly convincing and recalling him to the task at hand. She wanted a spanking, and by gosh, she would get one. If this was how she wanted to play it, let the games begin.

Chapter 3

How could a hand hurt so much? Again and again Liam's palm smashed down against Shea's ass, each stinging blow making her yelp with pain. His other hand was clamped against the back of her neck, pinning her to the bed. Almost as bad as the physical pain, was the confusion and humiliation. The engaging man she'd fallen for over dinner had morphed into a madman.

Had she somehow given the impression she *wanted* what was happening? Which part of *no* and *stop* did this asshole not get? Shea jerked hard beneath the man's iron grip and managed to twist her head back. "Liam, please stop! You're hurting me. Why are you doing this? Oh! Ow!"

"Because you're a very naughty girl, Shea. You need to be punished. You said so yourself."

"*I* said—huh?" What the *hell* was going on?

Liam pushed Shea's head down against the mattress. His hand crashed against her ass like a paddle, again and again and again. Shea could feel the tears wetting her face.

As the spanking went on and on, coherent thought and even language began to slip away, replaced entirely by feelings, some of which she couldn't begin to process. Finally, exhausted from the struggle and her terror, Shea went limp against the constant onslaught. He couldn't do this forever. Eventually he had to stop.

As she lay there in defeat, the oddest thing began to happen. Though Liam continued to smack her as hard as before, somehow it stung less, the pain shifting into a kind of heat that was almost pleasurable. The hand that had been holding her down was now stroking her back, its touch soothing. All resistance gone, Shea relaxed, her body sinking into the mattress, her muscles easing their clench.

"That's it," Liam said softly. "That's where I want you, Shea."

His hand nudged between her thighs. She had no strength to resist as Liam gently but insistently pushed her legs apart. He was still smacking her, though his touch was light now, almost sensual.

Shea tried to lift her head but found she couldn't move. She opened her mouth but no sound came, save for a long sigh. She was floating in a kind of altered consciousness, a place of deep peace like nothing she'd ever known. A tremor moved through her body when his fingers slid along the cleft of her pussy. She couldn't have closed her legs if she'd tried. When a finger slipped inside her, her sighs segued into moans.

Liam was doing something amazing with his hand. Shea was vaguely aware she should continue her struggle, but her muscles and bones had melted and her will seemed to have completely deserted her. Why fight against such peace, such pleasure?

She groaned as Liam continued to massage her clit from inside and out with his relentless, perfect touch. Her ass was on fire, but somehow the heat only served to intensify the feelings roiling inside her. She was panting, her hands clenched into fists, her toes curling. She heard a wail and was only dimly aware the sound had to be coming from her, as the strongest orgasm she'd ever experienced in her life crashed over her in wave after wave of pure sensation.

She must have lost consciousness, however briefly, because when she came to, she was cradled in strong arms. She opened her eyes and saw Liam smiling tenderly down at her.

"Hey, you," he said softly. "You floated away there. Are you okay?"

Shea's lips curled into a half smile as she stared into the handsome man's eyes. "Am I okay?" she echoed stupidly. He nodded and pulled her closer. She let herself drift. It felt good to be held like this. It felt safe.

Slowly the sensual fog lifted from her mind and she came more fully to herself. She winced as she shifted in the man's arms. The skin on her tender bottom felt as if it had been flayed. As her mind began to clear, her righteous anger resurfaced. Stiffening, she pulled herself from Liam's warm embrace and rolled to the bed beside him. She grabbed the edge of the coverlet and pulled it over her body as she glared at the man, daring him with her eyes to try and snatch it away.

He was regarding her with a bemused expression that made her angry as a wasp. "You bastard!" she cried. "This isn't funny!" Shea let all the fury and confusion that was boiling its way back into her brain burst into her voice. "You just tore off my clothes and spanked my ass until I cried and you have the nerve to ask if I'm *okay*? This is definitely *not* what I signed up for. I don't know what the fuck this Paradise Islands thinks it's doing, but I can tell you the lawsuit I plan to file will bankrupt you to hell and back for the next fifty years."

His expression of bemusement shifted to incredulity. "I don't understand." He shook his head, regarding her with a steady gaze. His voice took on a formal tone. "Forgive me for stepping out of character here, but what exactly is the problem, Ms. Devon? I was only following the dictates of your profile. You were very specific in your questionnaire about what a brat you are, and how you need to be taken in hand. You stated, and I quote, 'I need a good, hard spanking from a man willing and able to keep me in line.' If you were really having such a hard time, why didn't you use your safeword?"

Shea's mouth had fallen open. "My what? I need a *what*?" she sputtered indignantly. "What the hell are you talking about? I signed up for moonlight strolls on the beach and candlelit romance! Why in the world would I take a week out of my very busy life to be subjected to this" — she wrapped her arms tightly around herself — "this humiliation?"

Liam shook his head, his eyes narrowing as he regarded her with a furrowed brow. "Okay, let me get this straight. You're saying you *didn't* specifically ask for a spanking? That you *didn't* request BDSM role playing that included your pretending to resist while longing to surrender? Are you also denying that you, and again I quote, are seriously into erotic pain, and crave the whip, the crop, the cane and the paddle?"

Shea was struck speechless for several long seconds before she rallied enough to snap, "You bet I'm denying that — categorically denying every crazy thing you just said. I don't know whose questionnaire you were reading, but it sure as hell wasn't mine."

"Thank god," Liam muttered, which only served to confuse Shea further.

"What?" she demanded.

He stood abruptly. "There's been some kind of terrible mistake, Ms. Devon," he said, again using that formal tone. "I am very, very sorry. I've been operating under a grave misapprehension and I beg your pardon."

He bent down and retrieved her dress and panties, which he placed carefully on the bed beside her. "You should know I don't actually work directly for Paradise Islands anymore. I was hired on a freelance basis because of the particular fantasy you, or rather, whoever filled out that questionnaire, was requesting. I am a trainer by profession. I work with submissives and Dominants who are seeking a deeper level of understanding and commitment in the D/s lifestyle."

Shea stared Liam, trying to process what the heck he was saying. He continued, "Please, if you'll dress and come with me, we'll get to the bottom of this regrettable mistake." He glanced at his watch. "The boat won't be back until morning, so I'm afraid you're stuck here for the night."

Shea was still back on the earlier part of the conversation. "What did you say you were? A trainer? Like black leather and whips and chains type stuff? Is that what you're talking about?"

Liam offered a sardonic smile, though his expression remained troubled. "Yes, I guess you could characterize it that way, though sadomasochism is only a part of the D/s experience."

"D/s?"

"Dominance and submission. You've probably heard the acronym BDSM. I like to describe it as three interlocking parts of a whole. BD stands for bondage and discipline, then you have DS, for domination and submission, and finally SM, for sadism and masochism. For me personally, the real power lies in the D/s relationship, while bondage, discipline and erotic sadomasochism are subsets of the whole."

Shea reached for her panties and pulled them on beneath the shield of the sheet. Though her bottom still stung, she supposed she wasn't really the worse for wear. And that orgasm…

Shea grabbed her dress and pulled it over her head, feeling somewhat more in control now that she wasn't half naked. She shook her hair from her face and tilted her head to regard Liam. She hadn't been kidding about the lawsuit when she'd made the threat, but now she wasn't so sure. Clearly a mistake had been made, one that wasn't Liam's fault. He really did look quite stricken.

"Let me make you some tea," he offered in his lovely accent. This British suggestion made Shea smile. "And I can draw you a bath. A hot soak in the tub, a good night's sleep—of course I'll stay in the living room on the sofa." His face crumpled with genuine remorse. "Oh, Shea. I really am truly sorry. You must have thought me such a brute. I honestly believed I was giving you what you wanted. I am quite sure, once this is all sorted out, Paradise Islands will give you a full refund and a new fantasy packet of your choosing with their compliments. In fact, you have my word on it."

Liam held out his hand and Shea allowed him to help her from the daybed. She followed him out of the dungeon and through the living room into the kitchen, still feeling dazed. She sat gingerly at the table and watched as he put a kettle of water on the range and pulled two mugs from a cabinet. He got a lemon from the refrigerator and sliced it onto a plate, which he brought to the table, along with a small pot of honey.

The kettle whistled cheerfully. He poured the hot water over teabags and brought the mugs to the table. He slid onto the chair across from her and touched her arm, the concern evident in his face. "You aren't saying much. I do appreciate your calmness in the face of all this, I must say. But what's going on with you? Are you going to be okay, Shea?"

She nodded, realizing it was true. The shock and pain of the experience had been curiously and, if she were honest, powerfully offset by the stunning orgasm this virtual stranger had managed to pull from her. She wanted to understand more of what had happened. Thinking over the altered state she'd floated through toward the end of the bizarre experience, she had to wonder if it was just possible that the amazing orgasm hadn't necessarily been in spite of the spanking, but, at least partially, because of it.

Shea's mind was teeming with a jumble of confused thoughts. One thing she'd learned in the world of high powered financial negotiations—it was better to stay quiet until you knew what you wanted to say, rather than blurt out whatever was in your head. Keeping this in mind, she lifted the teabag from the steaming mug and set it on the small plate Liam had placed on the table for the purpose. She squeezed a wedge of lemon into her mug and stirred in a spoonful of honey.

She had to admit she liked the way Liam seemed to be calmly waiting for her to speak. Most people in this situation would either be babbling on about how they would fix things, or peppering her with questions in an attempt to do damage control. Instead, he was regarding her patiently with such somber focus. He must be freaking out, and yet his concern seemed to be entirely for her.

Shea took a sip of the strong, hot tea. Not quite ready to address the main issue at hand, she said, "You know, I didn't even book this vacation packet. Someone else bought it for me as a gift."

Liam raised his brows. "Really? That's quite a gift. These packages don't come cheap."

Shea nodded. "My boss, Jackie. Essentially it was a 'take a vacation or get fired' sort of ultimatum."

Liam smiled. "Rather an unusual choice, I must say."

"Yeah. Aside from thinking myself too indispensible to take the time"—Shea offered a rueful grin—"I was totally against it at first, this whole weird idea of purchasing a sexual fantasy. I mean, it smacks of the desperate, don't you think?"

"Oh, I don't know. From my experience when I worked for the company, it's really more about wish fulfillment—you know, making a fantasy come true, or at least as nearly true as possible, given the circumstances. Most women who buy the week are looking for something different, something fun and completely out of the realm of their day-to-day lives. Some women, and I had assumed you might be one of these, given your busy life and the demands of your career, are just looking for a week of, forgive my bluntness, wild sex with no strings attached. They get to spend a week in an exotic, luxurious locale and they know they're going to get a guy who is disease-free, reasonably attractive and there to lavish his attention on them and them alone."

"It is an interesting business model," Shea agreed, her banker mind turning over the investment potential of such a venture. "I wonder if there's ever been such a colossal fuckup as this, though. A company that is so careless with its clients can't have much staying power."

"Agreed," Liam replied. "Something went awry, and I'm sure Sylvia will get to the bottom of it. She's a real stickler for client confidentiality. I've never heard of anything like this happening in the company's five years of operation. But, as I'm sure you know from your own experience, a company is only as good as its support staff. It sounds as if some files must have gotten switched or something. I wonder if there's another poor woman on one of the other islands just waiting to be taken firmly in hand by her dream Master, while the guy she's actually with is trying to give her the moonlight and gentle kisses you signed on for."

Shea laughed. The bizarre episode in the dungeon notwithstanding, she had laughed more and enjoyed herself more in this man's company than with anyone she could remember. He wasn't only drop-dead gorgeous with a sexy accent, he was articulate, thoughtful, funny and considerate. And then there was that amazing orgasm…

"We'll get this settled in the morning," Liam said. "I'll call for the boat first thing in the morning so you can get back to your life."

Shea said nothing to this, refusing to admit how much his apparent eagerness to get rid of her stung. Yet, regardless of any feelings that did or didn't exist between them at this point, did she really want to jump on the next plane back to Houston, to face the gridlock traffic, the twelve hour workdays and the lonely nights? After all, the week was already bought and paid for.

Shea looked over her mug at the man sitting across from her, unable to deny that she wanted this man, whoever he was. What had gotten into her? Was she really going to fool herself into believing this was anything but an act? Was she going to be like those pathetic guys who believed the prostitute they'd hired for a quickie was actually "into them" for anything but their money?

Was this scenario really any different? This week was just another job for him, another lonely woman to service for a fee. Shea forced a mental shrug. After all, wasn't that what she had wanted? A casual fling with no strings attached?

She took another sip of her tea. "Let's sleep on it. Things always look different in the morning."

~*~

The night sky outside the bedroom windows was studded with a million diamond pinpricks. Shea was asleep beside Liam, her back to him, the sheet pulled over her slender form. Though sleep continued to elude him, he didn't mind just watching the lovely woman as she slept. He would have liked to take her into his arms and bury his face in her soft hair, but he restrained himself. They had agreed they would share the bed, nothing more.

Given the circumstances, he had been perfectly willing to sleep on the sofa, but Shea had insisted she didn't mind sharing the king-size bed. "It's not your fault the company got its wires crossed," she'd said magnanimously. When she slid between the sheets, the curves of her luscious body hugged by a satin nightie, he was glad he was already under the covers, his instant, pulsing erection hidden from view.

Back when he worked for Paradise Islands he would have been expected to service the client, even on the first night, if that was what they wanted. His particular role for the company as a trainer and Dom had given him more leeway than most of the guys working there, but in the end he, too, was just another hired hand, even if the nature of his services wasn't entirely sexual.

Given the strange situation, he no longer knew what was expected of him and so had let Shea call the shots. He was both confused and conflicted by what had transpired over the course of the evening. He couldn't deny his deep and immediate attraction to Shea Devon, and this in itself was unsettling. She hadn't committed yet to staying or leaving, though he was reasonably sure that, by the light of day, she would bolt, embarrassed by what had occurred, and by her explosive reaction to it.

That was the thing that was so intriguing. Based on her powerful response to the spanking and the orgasm he'd teased from her afterward, Shea clearly had strong masochistic and submissive leanings, and yet seemed entirely unaware of them, at least so she claimed. How had she managed to get this far in her life without even an inkling of what lay at the core of her sexuality?

He knew even as he pondered this that it was a stupid question. She was thirty-two, unmarried, and from what he could glean from their conversation over dinner, had never been in love. She was beautiful, intelligent, charming—so what was the problem? Clearly, the problem was that she was too shut down, too defended, too driven in other areas of her life to connect with the essence of her true nature. What she needed, and clearly had never found and probably never sought, was a man who could break down those barriers. A man who could penetrate the defenses she'd spent a lifetime erecting.

But he wasn't that man, surely. He was here with her by accident, because of a mistake made back at the Houston office when setting up Shea's fantasy week. He was a fool to think her reaction had anything to do with him as a man. No—she was reacting to what he had given her. He needed to remember that.

As a trainer, he had become very adept at keeping his desires and urges firmly under wraps. It wasn't appropriate or even fair to those he trained to interject his personal feelings. And when he'd been working for Paradise Islands there had been no question—he offered his full attention and his body, but never his heart, not even a little, not even once.

Even so, as a Dom, there was nothing more thrilling or empowering than when a sub slipped into that amazing place when erotic pain transcended itself and was reborn as something sublime. While watching Shea loosen and ease into that perfect space, Liam had been certain she was a natural. If she could react with such intense honesty and sensitivity without any training, just imagine what it would be like to guide her willingly along the path?

Yet, he was well aware it wasn't that simple. Despite a slowly gaining acceptance of BDSM into the mainstream, most people's understanding was limited to badly written erotica and tacky porn sites that depicted the "whips and chains type stuff" to which Shea had referred with such charming ignorance.

Shea uttered a small sigh as she rolled onto her back, still apparently asleep. Liam's arm was outstretched between them, and she shifted her head until it was resting against his biceps, her dark, shiny hair tickling his skin. He kept very still for several long moments, not wanting to wake her. Though he knew he would have been wiser to gently pull his arm away, turn over and go to sleep, instead slowly, carefully, he shifted closer and curled his arm just enough to move the sleeping girl into a light embrace.

She was warm beside him, her skin impossibly soft. Unable to resist, he nuzzled his cheek gently against her hair. She smelled like heaven—the light, floral scent of her shampoo mingling with the warmer undertone of a spicy perfume and the faint lingering scent of female musk. He wanted to gather her into a tight embrace and feel the press of her body against his. More than that, he wanted to roll on top of her and feel the soft, yielding curves of her luscious body beneath his. He wanted to fuck her. He wanted to make love to her.

Stop it. You've known her for a few hours. This is lust, infatuation, nothing more.

He almost believed it.

For the first time in a very long time, Liam stood on uncertain ground, unsure what came next, or even what he wanted. No. That was a lie. He knew what he wanted, and he'd been around long enough to know full well that didn't mean he'd get it.

Slowly, carefully, he extracted his arm from beneath Shea's head. Turning away from her, he closed his eyes and listened to the gentle, lulling sound of the waves lapping the shores of their tiny island.

Chapter 4

Shea opened her eyes, for a moment unsure where she was. The large bed was empty. Sunlight streamed in through the windows and she could hear the faint sound of the waves lapping against the shore through the hurricane glass.

She sat up and stretched as she looked out the windows to the beach beyond. She saw a figure of a man pacing along the shore, a cell phone pressed to his ear. Was Liam already on the phone with Paradise Islands straightening out the error? Was that what she wanted?

Pee. Shower. Coffee. That was what she wanted.

She glanced again at the tall man cast in silhouette against the glittering sea. She wanted him, too. There was no denying it.

When she came out of the bathroom to dress, she looked out the windows toward the shore. Liam was gone. A few minutes later she emerged from the bedroom, her hair still wet, her feet bare. She wore a pink silk tank top and black shorts, both purchased for this trip.

Walking to the kitchen, she found Liam at the table doing something on his smart phone, a cup of coffee at his elbow. He looked up with a smile. "Good morning. I trust you slept well?"

Shea nodded, surprised to realize she had. She'd been expecting to toss and turn the night before, with a strange man beside her, her bottom still tender from the spanking, her mind still reeling from the events of the day. Yet she must have crashed almost instantly, not stirring once till the morning.

"Like a log," she replied. "Must be all that fresh sea air." *Or that amazing orgasm.*

"Hopefully it gave you an appetite, too. I have some croissants in the oven. They should be about ready. I would be happy to make you some eggs, if you'd like." Liam stood and moved toward the range.

Shea had been about to say she never ate breakfast when he pulled open the oven door and the delicious buttery smell of the baked rolls filled the kitchen. Her mouth was watering and she swallowed. "Those smell wonderful."

"The catering company that services these islands does a really good job." Liam removed the cookie sheet from the oven and tilted it over a lined bread basket. He brought the basket, along with butter and a small pot of fruit preserves, to the table.

While Shea selected a croissant from the basket, he poured hot coffee into her mug. "Thanks," she said, inhaling the rich aroma of the coffee. "A girl could definitely get used to this."

Liam sat again across from her, flashing a quick, tight smile that didn't quite reach his eyes. "The boat should be here by noon, so you'll want to pack. I wasn't able to connect yet with Sylvia, but I left her a voicemail outlining the problem. I'm sure she'll get this straightened out at once."

"Wait. What?" Shea blurted, taken aback by his blunt declaration. "You already ordered the boat? Just like that?"

"Surely that's what you want? You were brought to BDSM island in error. We need to rectify the situation." Liam's expression was difficult to read, but his meaning was pretty clear. He was done. The week was over before it had begun.

What an idiot she'd been to think there could be anything between them. That spanking and what had followed, while mind-blowing for her, meant next to nothing to him. He'd been acting a part, and now that he had no role to play, he was ready to pack it in.

To hide her chagrin, and beneath it the hurt, she snapped, "I'm the client here, no? Seems to me I should be the one to make that decision, not you."

Liam lifted one eyebrow, his lips quirking into a half smile. "Seems to me the decision was made the moment I discovered you were brought here under false pretenses."

"It's my week. If I want to stay, I can stay," Shea insisted, annoyed to hear the petulance in her voice.

Liam's expression softened. He reached across the table and put his hand over hers. Just his touch sent an electric jolt through her body and Shea felt herself blushing. What was her problem? She pulled her hand from beneath his and reached for her mug, using it to hide her face as she took a sip of coffee.

"Shea, it's not going to work."

"What's not going to work?" she persisted. "I booked a week on this island. Are you telling me I can't stay here and use it?"

"Not at all. It's just" —he lifted his hands, holding them palms up over the table—"I don't work for Paradise Islands. No offense meant whatsoever to you, but I'm no longer willing to, uh, service women for money. I agreed to this week because it was my understanding that you were seeking a submissive experience. And based on your reaction in the dungeon, I do believe you have submissive potential, but by the same token, I understand you didn't sign up for this."

"Submissive potential?" Shea hid her confusion with indignation. "What the hell do you mean by that? I'm nobody's submissive. I structure deals worth hundreds of millions of dollars. I work with some of the top entrepreneurs in the country."

Liam smiled. "Please don't misunderstand me. I'm not talking about your prowess as a businesswoman. Nor did I intend to malign your character or insult you in any way. What I mean by submission is something entirely different. I was speaking in the sensual, interpersonal sense. The willingness and ability of one person to submit sexually, emotionally and physically to another person takes real courage. It takes total honesty and absolute trust. It's not a game to be casually played."

"Seems to me you were more than willing to play it as part of this BDSM packet you thought I'd signed up for," Shea retorted, though she couldn't deny she was intrigued by his words.

Liam nodded somberly. "Agreed, though I confess I had misgivings. Still, as a favor to Sylvia, I stepped in at the last minute when her Dom-in-residence was unable to be here. But after last night with you" — a sudden pain washed over his face that startled Shea with its intensity — "I realized I'm not up to the task."

Now she was really confused. "I'm sorry, what? Not up to the task? But you have to. You signed up for this. You're getting paid." That wasn't what she had wanted to say, not what she felt. What a jerk she was being. She pressed her lips together to keep from saying anything else stupid.

Liam blew out a breath. He placed his hands flat on the table and stared down at them. Finally he looked up, his deep brown eyes gazing intently into hers. "I can see I need to be completely honest with you, Shea. This is about more than you getting what you paid for, or me doing what I was paid to do."

Shea looked down, embarrassed. Reaching for her, Liam lifted Shea's chin by placing his forefinger beneath it. Shea drew back, startled by the gesture. "Though I hadn't meant for it to be the case, I find that there's more at stake here." Liam paused, as if girding himself for what he had to say. "Here's the thing. Last night when I was spanking you, and afterward when I brought you to orgasm"—Shea felt herself blushing hotly and she looked away to avoid his gaze as he continued—"I felt the power of your submission. And beyond that, I felt my answering need to dominate you—to claim you. It was, frankly, unexpected and not entirely welcome. Not within the context of this fantasy week in which we would both just be playing a part."

Taking his mug in hand, Liam stood from the table and moved toward the counter. He turned his back to her as he filled his cup. His words echoed through her mind—*the need to dominate you – to claim you*—and sent a shiver through her body. He turned back to face her, though he remained standing. "I think it's best, in the circumstances, that we both return to Houston."

"And what if I say no?"

"Excuse me?" Liam lifted his eyebrows.

"You've acknowledged this is *my* week," Shea pressed on. "Bought and paid for. I've cleared my schedule. Jackie would have my ass if I tried to show my face at the office before my vacation is over. We're already here on this gorgeous island. Before you realized they gave me the wrong packet, you were more than willing to commit to a week of 'servicing' me"—she drew quotation marks around the words— "so it seems to me, questionnaire confusion or no, that you *owe* me this week, Mr. Jordan."

"You think so, huh?" Liam's tone was amused. "Is that an order, Ms. Devon? Is that what you really want?"

"I—well, I..." Shea didn't really know what she wanted, beyond the fact that she didn't want to return to Houston, and she didn't want to say goodbye to Liam Jordan.

He sat again at the table. Reaching over, he took one of Shea's hands between his own, and her heart skipped a beat at his touch. "Listen, Shea. If I agreed to stay for the week with you—"

"If you agreed? It's my w—"

"Stop it," Liam cut in, startling Shea into silence with the firmness of his tone, though he didn't raise his voice. More gently, he added, "I'm not willing to be your, uh, sexual escort, for lack of a better term. That's not what I'm about. It wouldn't be fair to either of us."

Shea frowned. She wasn't used to being told no. She didn't like it. But beyond that, deeper than that, she was intrigued, if a little scared, by the idea of erotic submission.

"What if," she began in a tentative tone, her body tingling suddenly with the memory of that intense spanking and the subsequent powerful orgasm, "I *did* want to explore this submission thing you're talking about?"

Liam was quiet for several beats. "I'm not sure you understand what you're saying. What that would entail."

"So enlighten me then," Shea retorted, frustrated and a little embarrassed that he hadn't immediately leaped on the idea. Hadn't he been the one to claim he wanted to explore her submissive potential, as he called it?

This time his smile did reach his eyes, which crinkled merrily at the corners. "All right then. Here's the deal. If I were to agree to take you on for the week, it would be on my terms, not Paradise Islands' and most definitely not yours."

"Take me on?" It was Shea's turn to lift her brows.

Liam nodded. "That's correct. If I agree to stay here with you for the week, it will be as your trainer. You will be subject to my rules, and you will obey to the very best of your ability, or suffer the consequences."

"Oh, yeah. Right," Shea snorted and tried to grin. Was he nuts? Yet, beneath her cavalier dismissal was a sudden, intense yearning that nearly took her breath away.

Liam didn't grin back. He regarded her with a somber gaze. "Those are the terms, Shea. And I don't enter into them lightly. Nor should you. You already know I'm very attracted to you—I've told you as much with more than just words. But this isn't about that. What I'm offering you is a chance to connect with a part of your psyche I'm sensing has gone largely unexplored. And I believe, until you understand that part of yourself, and beyond that, learn to embrace it, you will remain unfulfilled."

Shea found herself mute as she waited for him to continue.

"Forgive me if I overstep," Liam went on, "but I'm willing to venture that you've never found the man who could meet the needs you hold deep inside—needs you haven't been able to articulate or even understand. Perhaps you've even given up on finding the kind of intensity in a relationship that you crave.

"I'm guessing you throw yourself into your work as a way to avoid the inevitable disappointment when yet another potential partner falls by the wayside of your expectations. I'm not saying you don't date or have men in your life." He gave a small, appreciative chuckle. "In fact, with your beauty and charm, I'm sure you have to fend them off with a stick. But what I mean is, you haven't found the one who makes your heart pound, the one who can connect on a level beyond language, beyond conscious thought, to that part of you that longs for something deeper, something more intimate than mere sex."

"And let me guess the next line," Shea quipped, letting the sarcasm ripple through her words to cover her discomfiture. "*You're* that man?" Even as she said this, she felt foolish. He was trying to express something important, and she was reacting like a defensive teenager.

His smile seemed sad, which made her feel even worse for the snarky comment. If she could have pulled the words back, she would have. "I'm sorry," she said quietly. "I'm not usually like this. You have me flustered."

"It's okay. Really. I'm throwing a lot at you. I don't mean to put you on the defensive. I just want you to understand that I know who you are. I know, because I'm the flip side of your coin. I spent years refusing to connect with that dominant part of my nature because I was confused about the difference between dominance and being a bully or a pig. It took me a while to figure out that inflicting erotic pain is a very different thing from raising a hand to a woman.

Accepting a consensual exchange of power is very different from taking what you want because you can. I didn't get to a new level of understanding by myself. There were people in the community, in the lifestyle, to guide and help me."

Liam again put his hand over hers and Shea turned hers so their palms were touching. "Wow. That sounds pretty intense. I barely know what you're talking about. This is all so new to me."

Liam nodded. "There are as many variations in the lifestyle as in any vanilla relationship. But underlying a true D/s connection is the understanding that, once the sub willingly and freely gives herself to her Dom, she abdicates her erotic freedom. The exchange of power is consensual, but also absolute. By the same token, the Dom's responsibility for the sub's wellbeing and his promise to love and cherish her submission is absolute."

Shea realized she had been holding her breath and she let it out with a sigh. The picture he painted sounded so romantic, but also so strange.

"Of course, we're just talking about a week of training. It's a taste, if you will, a chance for you to dip your toe in the waters and see if this is a path you want to explore. Under those conditions, I'm willing to give you a glimpse into what a D/s lifestyle entails. Not as a game, or part of a play vacation package, but as a true training experience. Frankly, I'm not sure how far we can go, given how new you are to the experience and given the constraints of a single week, but if you're interested, it's a place to start."

"I don't know what to say," Shea murmured, though her body seemed to know. She still didn't fully grasp everything he was saying, but every fiber of her being felt alive, nerve ends firing, blood pumping, skin tingling, heart pounding, nipples aching.

"It's your call, Shea," Liam continued. "It's your decision. Just be aware, if you say yes to the training, there's no going back. You don't call it quits the moment you find yourself embarrassed or resistant to something I require of you. It's a lot to ask, I get that. Maybe too much, since to make the experience meaningful, absolute trust is essential. It's the only way I could make this work, not just for you, but for myself."

Shea stared at the handsome man across the table, her mouth working, though no sound came. His cell phone began to chirp. "It's Sylvia," he said, looking down at the screen. "I'll just tell her we're discussing options, shall I?"

Mutely, Shea nodded, glad of the momentary reprieve.

Liam picked up the phone, swiped his finger over the screen and lifted it to his ear. Hi, Sylvia." Shea could hear a woman's voice speaking rapidly through the receiver. "Yes, that's right. There was a mix up."

He paused as another torrent of feminine sound burst through the phone. "I will let her know. Of course. Full refund. New week. Yes, I understand. But I have a question for you. Ms. Devon and I are discussing some alternate possibilities at the moment. Listen, if we do decide to move forward with the week, that's not a problem, correct? No one else is booked for the island?" He paused to listen and then smiled. "Excellent. I'll let you know of our decision within the hour. Yes, yes. I do appreciate that. I will tell her. Okay, I'll get back to you soon. Thanks. Bye."

He replaced the phone on the table and leaned back in his chair. "I am to pass on her heartfelt apologies. She hopes you will stay for the week, and wants you to know you have a free week waiting whenever you're ready to rebook. Meanwhile, she's fine with us using this island for the week. It's up to you. If you agree, I'll call Scott and let him know we won't need his services until he brings fresh supplies mid-week. But remember, if you say yes, you're agreeing to a week of intensive D/s training. This won't be an act and neither of us will be playing a part.

"I take what I do very seriously, and I will expect no less from you. The word *no* will not exist in your vocabulary. This doesn't mean I'm going to force you to do things you are uncomfortable with or afraid of. I will ascertain and respect your limits as a part of the process. But you need to know that if you commit to this process, I will be the one to decide everything you do, or do not do, for the duration of the week. So, what will it be, Shea Devon? Yes, or no?"

Shea stared at Liam, her thoughts racing. Could she do all that he seemed to be asking of her? Did she want to? Was she crazy to even consider it? Better to let Scott pick her up and take her away from this tiny island and this whole bizarre scenario. If she wanted to try this training thing with Liam, she could always look him up once she was back in Houston. She could do it in her own time, on her own terms.

Or not. She could go back to her life—her familiar, comfortable, lonely, quiet life that consisted of work and sleep and little else.

Maybe he was just making it all up—this so-called sense he had of her submissive potential, whatever the fuck that really was. So, she got off on that spanking, so what? That didn't mean she was seeking some intense lifestyle as someone's sex slave, for heaven's sake. That stunning orgasm had lowered her resistance, that was all that was going on here. Liam Jordan's sexual skill and sheer animal magnetism were muddling her brain. She wasn't thinking clearly. She couldn't seem to make up her mind.

Liam reached across the table and drew his thumb in a sensual line down Shea's cheek. His eyes seemed to be looking past hers and right into her secret thoughts. She felt naked beneath his penetrating gaze. Her heart was pounding. Her mouth was dry and she couldn't seem to catch her breath. Her rational mind told her to refuse. The part of her brain that was still functioning instructed her to offer a dismissive laugh and a flat-out *no*.

She opened her mouth to speak.

"Yes," she whispered. "Yes."

Chapter 5

Liam tilted his head as he gazed at the lovely young woman sitting across from him. Her cheeks were flushed, her pupils dilated, her lips softly parted. He could see she was both excited and frightened by the word she had whispered, almost as if it had escaped from her mouth without her express permission. Did she really want this? Did she really understand what she had just signed up for?

"I'll cancel the boat, then, shall I?" Liam said, giving her a last chance to change her mind, refusing to allow himself to acknowledge how much he prayed she would not.

Shea nodded, though she looked as nervous as a cat.

"Shea. It's not too late. You can still change your mind."

A resolute, stubborn look came over her face as she thrust out her chin and squared her shoulders. Liam smiled. He loved her fire and had no intention of quenching it. Submission from a place of confidence and power was the ultimate aphrodisiac in his book. "Cancel it," she said in a forceful tone. Yet when she reached for her coffee, Liam noticed the slight tremble of her hand.

He picked up his phone and typed out a rapid text to Scott, who responded a moment later, acknowledging he would see them later in the week. He sent another to Sylvia, telling her they would be staying for the week, and he would be in touch. That done, Liam returned his focus to Shea. "Would you like another croissant or anything else before we get started?"

Shea wrapped her arms protectively around her torso, her fingers gripping knuckle-white into her upper arms. She pressed her lips together as if she was girding herself to leap off a tall building with no net below.

"Hey," Liam said gently, smiling, "it's going to be fine. I don't expect perfection off the bat, don't worry. I don't expect anything, really. We've identified a penchant, a desire within you, and this week will be about exploring and nurturing that desire and seeing if we can't, together, allow it to flourish into something meaningful. You okay with that?"

Shea seemed to relax a little, her fingers easing their death grip, her lips almost curving into a smile. "To be perfectly honest, I'm not sure I know what I'm doing, Liam. I know something happened last night that I want to understand better, but I don't really know what you're talking about or what to expect." She gave a small, nervous laugh. "Shit, if this was a business transaction, I just signed a contract without reading the fine print."

Liam nodded. "Let's take a walk on the beach. I'll explain my expectations and the framework of the week more thoroughly for you. Feel free to ask any questions. I need to keep in mind that you're a complete novice to the lifestyle, so things I might take for granted will be new to you." He stood and held out his hand, pleased when Shea slipped her hand into his as she rose. He tried not to stare at the lush curve of her breasts beneath her top, the hint of her nipples outlined against the silk. He needed to keep the focus on the training.

The warm, salty air greeted them as they stepped outside, the sun making the white sand and blue sea look as if they had been burnished with gold. They strolled along quietly for a while, moving closer to the waves to walk on the wet sand with their bare feet. A lot of women at this point would be chattering nervously. Liam liked that Shea stayed quiet, not because she was timid, but because she was waiting with patience and grace that would stead her well if she ever truly embraced a D/s lifestyle.

"The first thing we need to establish," Liam began, "is that I'm running this show, not you. I decide what we do, when we do it, how we do it and when we stop. You have input, of course, but ultimately it's up to me. Are we clear on that?"

Shea shrugged, keeping her eyes straight ahead as they walked. "Sure, yeah. You're the expert. I'm here to learn."

"Good. That's key. I direct. You obey."

"Got it," Shea said briskly, a worry line furrowing between her brows. Jesus, she was cute.

Forcing himself to remain focused, Liam continued, "We'll start out with a series of exercises designed to help me ascertain where you are right now in terms of your submissive sensibilities as well as your sensitivity and receptivity to erotic pain."

Shea drew in a sharp breath, her stride quickening. Liam caught up to her. "What is it?" Shea didn't reply. Liam took her arm, pulling her to a stop. "Shea, listen to me. One of the first things we need to establish is an open line of communication. I am not one of those 'you will only speak when spoken to' kind of Doms. Especially not during the training process. I need to hear from you openly and often. You need to tell me how whatever is happening affects you. That doesn't mean I'll necessary stop what I'm doing, but I need to know what's going on with you if there seems to be an issue."

Shea faced him and he let go of her arm. "Okay, then," she said. "Pain. Erotic pain. What the hell *is* that? I mean, yeah, something happened after that blistering spanking, but during it, I fucking *hated* it! It hurt! What's erotic about that?"

They began to walk again. "It's a good question, Shea, and I'll answer it the best I can. The word pain is a loaded one. Really, I should use the word *sensation* instead, to take away the stigma. Now, some masochists truly seek pain just for its sake. They get off on the act itself, on the sensation of something striking the skin, taking comfort in being tightly bound in rope or chain."

Shea's wildly skeptical look nearly made him laugh out loud. Could she really be so naïve about everything to do with BDSM? Maybe that wasn't a bad thing. She came to this experience with no preconceived notions or expectations. It was up to him to make it safe for her to succeed, or sometimes, to fail.

Liam continued his line of thought. "For others, the pain is more of a vehicle to get them where they want to go. It's a kind of gauntlet they must run through to get to the prize at the end. Especially for those new to the scene, the concept of erotic pain is frightening, and fear can get in the way of the true experience. That's something we'll work through together."

"I don't know." Shea's tone was doubtful.

"That's okay. You don't have to. That's my job."

Shea stopped again and faced him with a scowl. "I'm not used to this, Liam. I like to be in control."

Liam laughed. "Spoken like a true sub. I can honestly say, I've never known a submissive who didn't like, or no, demand to be in control of just about every aspect of his or her life. Perhaps that's part of the deep appeal of erotic submission. For once, just once in your life, you get to give up that control. I'm not saying this is you, necessarily, but, just for the sake of argument, erotic submission allows one to relinquish that death grip on every detail of one's life. You get to let go. You can just *be*."

Shea didn't look entirely convinced, but her scowl softened a little and she nodded. "I guess that makes a kind of sense."

They turned around, having already walked nearly the length of the tiny island. "We'll get to the erotic pain soon enough," Liam said, "but first I want to get a better sense of some basic things, like how well you can listen and obey. That can be quite a stumbling block, especially at the beginning."

Shea stopped again. "What do you mean? How hard could that be? You say do X, and I do X." She was squinting a little in the sun, her lips pursed in question, her hands on her hips. She looked utterly adorable and Liam wanted to kiss her in the worst way.

You're her trainer, not her lover, he reminded himself sternly.

"I'll show you by example. Take off your top and bra and place them on the sand."

Shea looked nonplussed. "What?"

"You didn't hear me?"

"I heard you."

"But you haven't acted. Earlier you said you understand the dynamic between us. I am your trainer. I gave you a direct command but you're still standing there. What's that about?"

"Wait, what? You expect me to take off my clothes right here? Right now?" She looked wildly around the beach and out to sea, as if someone might be arriving at any moment.

Liam nodded, hiding his smile. "Right here. Right now." He stared her down, silently daring her to refuse. Shea stared back for several defiant seconds. Not a particularly auspicious start, but Liam let it pass. Eventually she looked away. Liam waited, watching. Finally she reached for the hem of her top and lifted it over her head. Shaking her shiny dark hair free, she dropped the top onto the sand.

He saw the flash of nervousness in her brief glance as she reached behind her back to unclasp the lacy pink bra, but to her credit, she continued. As the bra fell away, Liam drew in a breath and then pressed his lips together to keep from moaning in appreciation. Her breasts were perfect—high and round with dark pink nipples jutting out in the sea breeze.

Again putting her hands on her hips, Shea fixed him with a defiant, decidedly non-submissive stare, but the splash of color moving over her cheeks belied her bravado. Liam allowed his smile to surface. He let his gaze move over her body for several long seconds. While the color in her cheeks deepened, he was pleased to note she didn't attempt to hide her body from his scrutiny.

Satisfied, he said, "Good. If I were handing out marks for performance, you'd get a C+."

"C+?" Shea looked outraged. "What the hell? I did what you said, didn't I?"

"You did, eventually, which is why you didn't get an F. But you questioned me instead of just doing what you were told, and you hesitated. Plus you didn't follow the directions to the letter. When I give a command, you pay attention to every part of it, not just what suits you."

"What?" Again the scowl. "You said to take off my top and bra. I did that."

"I said to place them on the sand. Not drop them in a heap."

Shea glanced down at the small pile of clothing. "Oh. Well." She started to bend down, presumably to retrieve the items.

"I didn't tell you to do that. Stand at attention, arms locked behind your back. That means you cross your arms and grip each elbow with the other hand."

"Come on, you can't be serious." Clearly, she was pressing the envelope, seeing how much she could get away with.

"Shea. Do as you're told or you'll be punished."

"Punished! Wh—"

Liam gripped her shoulders and looked down into her pretty face. "This isn't a game, Shea. If you persist in defying me like this at every turn, it's not going to be worthwhile to either of us. It's not too late. I'll call Scott and you can be back in Houston by this afternoon."

He dropped her shoulders and turned away. He hadn't been making an idle threat. Yes, he was wildly attracted to Shea Devon, but he wouldn't subject either of them to a constant tug-of-war of wills. If she wasn't serious about the training, it was better to find out now and end the charade. With a heavy heart, he began to walk back toward the bungalow.

He couldn't deny the flood of relief when she called his name. "Liam! Come back. I'm sorry, okay? This is just a lot to handle, you know? I'm sorry. Please. Give me another chance."

Liam turned back. She was standing at attention, though her torso was swaying with the effort of gripping her arms as he'd commanded. He returned to stand in front of her, waiting until she was still. "I refuse to engage in a battle of wills with you, Shea.

This means too much to me to play around. Is that understood?"

She looked down. "Yes," she said softly, and then, to his astonishment, "Yes, sir."

~*~

Where had *that* come from? Shea never called anyone *sir* or *ma'am*. She considered herself anyone's equal, from the CEO of a Fortune 100 company to the boy who bagged groceries at the supermarket. Yet the word had popped unbidden out of her mouth, drawn from the same secret, dark place from which the word *yes* had been pulled when he'd asked if she wanted to stay.

Now she was standing here half-naked outside for anyone to see, her bare breasts thrust lewdly toward him as a result of the uncomfortable position she was in, her fingertips straining to reach each opposite elbow behind her back, and addressing this man who was only a few years older than she as *sir*. Yet somehow the appellation seemed correct. There was something dominant, no, more than that, something *masterful* about Liam that made her *want* to call him sir.

"Pick up your things and follow me," Liam said. When she looked up, he was already striding back toward the bungalow. Bending quickly, Shea reached for her clothing and scooped it up, pressing it against her bare torso as she watched the tall man moving away.

This whole thing still didn't feel entirely real. Though she would have denied it, he had kind of hit the nail on the head when he'd said she was just playing around. She had been testing him, and herself, she supposed. Though she wasn't particularly shy about her body, it had been disconcerting to be ordered to strip right there in the open. She had stalled for time, even though she knew he was testing her obedience.

Obedience!

Just the word rubbed her the wrong way. She hadn't got to where she was in her career by meekly bowing her head and doing what she was told. If that were the case, she'd still be a lowly bank clerk in a back office somewhere, instead of working for one of the top investment banking firms in Texas and pulling down a six figure salary, not to mention her sizable annual bonus.

Even as Shea tried to muster these thoughts in a show of false courage, she was a little ashamed of how she'd behaved. She could see that Liam was truly passionate about this thing he called the D/s lifestyle, and it wasn't fair to string him along like that, even if she'd only been doing it to hide her own nervousness. She would do better, she silently promised herself as she scurried to catch up with Liam. She owed it not only to Liam, but to herself.

When she followed him back through the French doors into the bedroom, he stopped her just inside. "Take off your shorts and panties. Fold all your clothes neatly and place them on top of the bureau."

Shea swallowed, thinking just how hard it was to get naked while the other person was fully clothed. Liam was watching her. "What?" he demanded. "Tell me what you're thinking."

Why not? He wanted to know what was going on in her head? Fine, she would tell him. "Okay. I'm wondering why you're ordering me to get naked while you remain fully clothed. It puts me at a disadvantage, you know?" She peered at him. "Huh, maybe that's what you *want*. You want me at a disadvantage so you can feel more powerful than me. More the one in control. Is that it?"

Liam shook his head, furrowing his brow though he offered a small smile at the same time. "I am the one in control. Now, do as you're told."

Something in his tone skipped past Shea's brain and went directly to her hands, which dutifully reached for her shorts. Frustrated that she couldn't control the rush of heat moving over her throat and face, she folded her things and placed them neatly on the bureau. Turning back, she stared at Liam, waiting.

"Stand at attention as before, gripping your elbows behind your back."

Shea obeyed, lifting her chin to hide her discomfort at being naked and on display. She felt as if she were a rubber band being pulled more and more taut. But damn it, she could do this! Liam was clearly challenging her with these demands, and Shea Devon had never backed away from a challenge. She wasn't about to start now.

She endured his slow, sweeping gaze of her body, keeping her head held high, though she had never felt so vulnerable in her life. *You can do this. You can do this. Don't give him the satisfaction of failing this simple task.* To her embarrassed dismay, her lower lip trembled and unwelcome tears pressed behind her eyes.

Without speaking, Liam stepped closer and reached for her face. He gently cupped her jaw in his palm, his fingers brushing her cheek. Shea leaned into his warm, comforting touch. She closed her eyes, willing her tears to remain unshed. This was stupid. Ridiculous. Why did she feel so wound up inside? And what the fuck was this tearing up nonsense? She never cried. What the hell was going on?

"Shea," Liam said, his tone kind, "easy does it. We're just beginning this exploration together. This isn't about me putting you at a disadvantage or anything like that. For this week, I'm your trainer. I'm not your adversary. I'm here to help you connect with something deep inside you. In order to do that, we have to break down certain barriers I sense you've spent a lifetime erecting."

He stepped back and reached around her, pulling her arms from behind her back as he moved closer. To Shea's surprise, he put his arms around her and gently drew her into an embrace, guiding her head to his chest. She couldn't stop the shuddering sigh that escaped her lips. She felt suddenly bereft of touch — both physical and emotional. The stark, frightening realization opened like a chasm at her feet, a yawning, dark loneliness she rarely permitted herself to acknowledge. She blinked back the renewed rush of hot tears pricking at her eyelids.

"Maybe I'm expecting too much, too fast," Liam said, his mouth close to her ear. "I've never worked with someone so completely new to the scene. We'll take it slower, okay? But for this to work, I need you to let go. I need you to stop resisting me each step of the way. I guess what it really comes down to is a matter of trust. You have to find a way to trust, Shea. Trust that I know what I'm doing. Trust that I won't take you where you don't ultimately long to go."

Just hold me like this forever, she thought, bringing her arms around him to keep him there. She had the odd sensation that if he released her, she would go flying off into space. As if he'd heard her silent plea, he pulled her closer and moved his strong hands soothingly over her back. She had to force herself to concentrate on his words and not let herself be overwhelmed by the feel and scent of his strong, warm body pressed against hers. She gripped him more tightly.

"Don't let me go. Please. Oh!" The words she'd only meant to think had just popped out of her mouth like the toads that fell out of the girl's mouth in a dimly-recalled fairy tale from her childhood.

"I have you, sweetheart," Liam whispered. "I know what it is to be lonely. I do."

His words burst through the already crumbling dam of her control, and Shea began to cry. Tears coursed down her cheeks and her shoulders began to shake. She didn't want to do this! She didn't want to cry. This was horrible. It was weak. It was stupid. He would definitely send her away now. Oh shit, shit, shit.

But she couldn't stop. Each gasping attempt to stuff the feelings back where they belonged only resulted in another gurgling, wet sob. He held her closer, whispering gently, "That's it, baby. Just let it go. Let it all go. I'll keep you safe. I promise."

As he spoke, he lifted her into his arms. He carried her to the bed and lay her gently down while she continued to sob like a baby. He lay beside her and again wrapped his arms comfortingly around her. He held her close, not even seeming to care that she was soaking his shirtfront with tears and snot.

Finally the river of tears slowed to a trickle, her sobs snuffling to a hiccup and a sigh. She should feel horrible for acting like a total idiot, but she was too exhausted to summon the emotions. It was as if a tightly coiled spring she hadn't even realized was wound inside her had sprung loose. Relief washed over her, as vast and deep as the ocean outside the bungalow.

"Rest now. Close your eyes and sleep."

A smile lifted the corners of her mouth as she followed Liam's sweet command and drifted peacefully away.

Chapter 6

Shea opened her eyes. A soft breeze moved the white curtains, beyond which stretched an endless, peaceful blue. She was naked beneath soft sheets. She brought her hand to her face. Her eyelids felt heavy and swollen and she pressed her fingers lightly against them.

"I have something better."

Startled, Shea whipped her head toward the sound of Liam's voice. He was sitting in a wingback chair near the windows. He stood and she saw he was shirtless, his broad, muscular chest covered in a fine down of golden hair. His hair was wet and slicked back, his cheeks kissed by sun. How long had she been asleep?

He moved toward the bed and sat down beside her. She could smell the ocean on his skin. "This will soothe you." He held out a white washcloth.

Shea smiled gratefully as she allowed Liam to drape the cool, wet washcloth over her closed eyes. When was the last time someone had done something so simple yet so caring for her? She honestly couldn't remember. "That does feel good. Thank you."

She lay quietly, glad for the cloth partially obscuring her face. What was going to happen now? Liam had stressed several times that it took courage and strength to submit. She'd definitely blown it when she'd broken down like a baby. He'd probably already called Scott to bring the boat back to the island.

"What time is it?" she asked, not wanting to deal with anything just yet.

"It's nearly two in the afternoon." Liam chuckled. "I was beginning to wonder if you ever planned to wake up. You slept like a log."

"Two o'clock!" Shea yanked the cloth from her face and sat up, pulling the sheet to keep her bare breasts covered as she faced Liam. "I never, ever sleep during the day. No way it's that late. Are you sure?"

Liam smiled and pointed to the small digital clock on the bedside table. "Clearly, your body needed the rest. You want some lunch?"

Before you send me away?

Shea snorted, not even trying to hide the bitterness in her tone. "Guess I really blew it, huh? It's over before it even started."

Liam looked confused. "What's over?"

Jesus, was he really going to make her spell it out? "The training," she blurted. "I fucked it all up. I broke down like some kind of lunatic for no reason whatsoever. I proved I'm not strong and courageous like a true sub, or whatever the hell it is you said I had to be." Fresh tears sprang to her eyes, which was beyond absurd, since she'd already cried away a lifetime's allotment of tears. Angrily she blinked them back. "The really stupid thing is, whether you believe it or not, I haven't cried since I was five." She shrugged helplessly. "I don't cry. Ever."

"Oh, Shea." Liam pushed her gently back against the pillows. He stroked her cheek, his words infused with tenderness. "Crying isn't a sign of weakness. What made you think that? It's just a release. You had a lot to process. I take some responsibility—I was moving too fast, I'm afraid." He smiled at her.

Helplessly, she smiled back. "So—so you aren't going to send me away?"

He shook his head. "No, you silly girl. Please, stop trying so hard to control this process. There's no script. There's no right or wrong. Just let things flow where they need to go. I'll be here every step of the way to guide you, I promise."

He bent toward her and Shea felt her heart give a lurch as his lips met hers. "Oh," he said softly, surprise in his voice, as if he hadn't meant to kiss her, hadn't known he was going to. When he started to pull back, impulsively Shea reached for him, not wanting him to stop.

Keeping his mouth over hers, he stretched out alongside her, pulling the sheet from her bare body as he drew her close. His skin was warm against hers. She could feel her nipples hard and tingling against his bare chest. His tongue ran along her lips, as if willing them to part. Shea opened her mouth in eager surrender. As his tongue danced with hers, his gentleness edged into something more insistent and Shea felt herself responding in kind.

He rolled on top of her, pressing her against the mattress with his weight. His mouth still on hers, he reached for her arms. Catching her wrists, he pulled her arms over her head, holding them down against the pillows as he continued to kiss her.

Shea felt as if the breath had been sucked from her body. Instinctively she pulled against Liam's grip, struggling beneath him as she tried to twist her head away. His hold on her tightened and he spread her arms wider apart, pinning them to the bed as he moved his mouth from her lips to her neck. His teeth nudged at her throat and she gasped in startled surprise.

Yet, even as Shea struggled beneath him, her cunt flooded with a wet, throbbing heat. Liam's cock rose beneath the thin fabric of his shorts and she experienced a spasm of need so stark and immediate it took her breath away.

Liam slid one strong thigh between her legs, forcing them apart. His fingers were tight around her wrists, his cock like a bar of iron pressing hard against her thigh. "Please," she panted. What was happening? Instead of outrage at being held down, Shea was more turned on, more excited, than she had ever been in her life.

"Please, what?" Liam's tone was teasing, even taunting. Again he bit her neck just where it met the shoulder, his tongue licking over the spot grazed a moment before by his teeth.

"Fuck me," Shea burst out before she could stop herself. Oh my god, had she actually said that out loud?

Liam gave a primal growl. "Is that what you want, Shea. You want my cock inside you? Hmmm?"

"Yes," she gasped as he dipped his head to her breasts. She groaned as his lips, teeth and tongue worked in tandem to create a confusing sensation of pleasure and pain so exquisite she thought she might come just from his mouth on her nipple.

He let go of her wrists as he moved over her, reaching down to yank off his shorts. Shea didn't move her arms from over her head, but simply lay there, waiting to be taken. Liam reached into the night table drawer and Shea suddenly realized what he was doing. "No," she whispered, and then louder, "No. I don't want it. Please."

He had grabbed a condom packet, which he now held between them. His eyes were boring into hers, the question clear on his face. Normally cautious in the extreme, Shea would never have imagined herself saying no to a condom, even though she was on the pill.

But this was different. Liam didn't feel like a stranger. Shea found she wanted, no—she needed—to feel his cock inside her without any sheathe that might keep him, even a little bit, apart from her.

She grabbed the condom from Liam's fingers and tossed it away. "I'm protected," she whispered as she reached for him, pulling him back down onto her.

Liam lifted himself over her, again reaching for her wrists. As he caught them once more in a tight hold, he parted her legs with his thigh. She whimpered as the head of his hard, thick cock nudged against her opening. He pushed forward and it felt as if her cunt were sucking him in, clutching his shaft in a spasm of raw, wet need.

"Oh, god," she moaned. Maddeningly, he lifted himself, nearly pulling out of her. Reflexively she arched her hips up, desperate to keep him inside her. She tried to pull her arms free so she could grab him and force him down onto her and into her. Easily holding her down, Liam gave a low, wicked laugh as he continued to tease her with just the head of his cock.

Shea opened her eyes to find Liam staring down at her, his deep brown eyes glittering with lust, his white teeth caught on his full lower lip.

"Please," she whispered urgently, again arching up to him.

"Beg me," he said hoarsely.

Shea felt a rush of humiliation—she begged no one for anything. And yet, at the same time, her cunt again spasmed with need, and raw desire washed over and through her, leaving her breathless and aching. "Please!" she cried, surrendering. "Please fuck me! Please, Liam, please, sir, fuck me, fuck me, fuck me! I'm begging you!"

His cock plunged, filling her almost painfully as he fell upon her. He began to thrust inside her, his fingers still digging into her wrists held high overhead. Shea felt an actual gush of wetness inside as her vaginal muscles spasmed and clutched at Liam's cock with each perfect thrust.

She had heard of vaginal orgasms, aware they had something to do the stimulation of the inner side of the clitoris, which was actually much larger than just the tip that emerged on top of the vulva, but she had never herself experienced one. Until now.

It started with a slow, quiet rumble, like a volcano thought to be extinct suddenly coming to life. Then it was if her entire body was melting, heated to a fever pitch by his hard body crushing hers against the bed, by his hands on her wrists, by his mouth on hers, by his cock thrusting in such perfect motion inside her. She began to keen—a high-pitched wail that had nothing to do with mourning and everything to do with pure, bright, perfect release.

Each thrust brought another animal cry of release as Shea writhed beneath Liam's masculine hold. His skin grew hot, as if a fire inside him had flared suddenly to life. He gasped in syncopated time against her uncontrollable cries of ecstasy as he jerked several times in rapid succession before collapsing heavily against her, his hands finally loosening their grip on her wrists.

They lay that way for several long moments, their skin slick with sweat, their hearts rat-a-tat tapping between them. Finally Liam rolled away from Shea. Lying beside her, he took her face in his hands as he looked into her eyes.

"I'm sorry, Shea. I didn't mean to do that. I had only meant to be your trainer. Not your lover. I don't know what happened." He shook his head with a small, rueful smile.

Shea lifted herself on one elbow. "Hey, no need to apologize. There's no script, remember? There's no right or wrong. Just let things flow where they need to go." She quoted Liam's words back to him. He grinned, and then they were both laughing, not just chuckling, but all-out guffawing, until the tears ran down their cheeks as they chortled with unbridled glee.

Finally they both quieted, save for the occasional lingering chuckle. Liam pulled Shea once more into his arms. "Let's have some lunch," he said. "You'll need your energy for what I have planned for you. We'll be spending the afternoon in the dungeon."

~*~

"In addition to getting a measure of your tolerance for erotic pain, I want to get a sense of how you handle being bound. Which brings me to the concept of a safeword. Are you familiar with that term?"

Shea shook her head. "Not really."

Liam had allowed her to put on a sundress while they ate lunch, though he hadn't allowed panties or bra. She looked so pretty and vulnerable standing there, biting her lower lip, her hands twisting nervously together. He would teach her how to be still as a part of her grace training, but for now he let her fidget.

"During a BDSM scene," he explained, "things sometimes move past the comfort zone of the submissive, so far past it that the scene needs to end then and there. Because of the nature of a Dom/sub relationship, sometimes just saying, 'no' or 'stop' might not work, because I could misinterpret that as you having difficulty or being afraid, but not *really* wanting things to stop. My subs very rarely need to employ a safeword, but that's because I really pay attention to their reactions, and I'll bring down the intensity if that's indicated."

Shea's eyes were wide and she gulped audibly. Liam wanted to pull her into his arms and kiss her, but reminded himself he was her trainer at this moment, not her lover. "But if, for some reason," he continued, "I don't seem to be getting it, and you really can't tolerate what is happening, you would use your safeword. It's a word you'll choose that's easy to remember, something neither of us will confuse for anything else. Just be aware that once you use that word, all action stops instantly. If you're bound, I'll release you as quickly as I can. The scene will stop and you'll have a kind of time out. Are you with me so far?"

"I think so. It's like saying *red light*, or something, right?"

"That's right." Liam nodded. "Since that's what pops into your mind, let's make that your safeword, shall we? If things get too intense for you at any point, you need to say *red light*. But I must caution you, a safeword is a last resort, only to be used when you feel you aren't getting through to your trainer or Dom and you really, desperately *need* whatever is happening to stop instantly."

"Jesus, Liam, that sounds kind of dangerous! What do you plan to do to me, that I'd be freaking out like that?" She cast an anxious look around the dungeon, her eyes flicking toward the cross where he'd bound her the night before, when he'd thought she was just playing the part of a willful brat.

"I don't expect you will need a safeword with me, Shea. Even if things get very intense, I am quite aware you're brand new to all this," he reassured her. "Safewords are more for seasoned participants who are able to tolerate high levels of erotic pain and confinement. I envision this week as just a taste of what you can expect, in the event you choose to embrace the lifestyle. Nevertheless, I want you to be aware and armed with your own word, just in case. Oh," he added, "if you can't speak, you will use a hand gesture. A good basic one is just to make a fist, and then open and close your fingers, like this." He demonstrated.

Shea stared down at his hand and then looked up at his face. "If I can't *speak*?" Her eyes had widened in such a comical expression of alarm that Liam couldn't stop his smile.

He shrugged. "If you were, say, gagged. Or maybe you had a leather hood over your head. That may sound odd to you at this point, to have some of your senses compromised, but it can be very freeing and can actually heighten the experience." At her doubtful expression, Liam added, "Don't worry about all this right now. It'll make more sense to you as we move through the training process." Shea said nothing, though she continued to worry her lower lip.

"The first thing to remember is trust," Liam continued. He thought of the wild, lustful look in her eyes when he'd held her down and she'd literally begged him to fuck her. But he understood that needing that kind of sexual control and release didn't necessarily translate into the total trust necessary during BDSM training. "You need to trust your trainer. So I need to pose that question directly to you now, Shea. Answer honestly, because without trust, we can't move forward. Do you trust me? Do you believe I will keep you safe during this process?"

"*Yes*. Yes. I trust you."

Liam was gratified by the speed and force of her response. He made a silent promise to be worthy of her trust. Aloud he said, "Thank you, Shea. Submission is a gift, and it's one I cherish when it's offered to me." Shea smiled at this, and again Liam made a silent promise to be worthy of her gift, even if it was only offered for this week.

"Now," he said, willing himself to slip fully into his role as trainer. "You will strip and stand at attention as you did this morning, arms behind your back, hands gripping each opposite elbow, legs spread shoulder-width apart. I am going to inspect your body, and while I'm doing so, I'll test your reaction to certain stimuli."

Though he could feel her nervousness, Shea did as she was told, shimmying out of the dress and letting it puddle on the floor at her feet. Her pussy was covered with a small, neat patch of dark pubic hair. Though he still found her breathtakingly lovely in her natural state, if she'd been his personal sub, he would have shaved her before they began, as he believed being fully bare heightened a sub's sense of vulnerability and accessibility.

He watched Shea put her arms behind her back as she assumed the at-attention position. He reached for her shoulders, adjusting her stance. "Spread your legs farther apart." He flicked lightly at her ankle with his toe and Shea obeyed, all the time staring up at him with those hauntingly lovely eyes.

Liam's cock throbbed in his shorts. He let his eyes move slowly over the beautiful naked young woman standing before him, amused as the color once again flooded her cheeks. Though they'd just made love, she was shy about her body, despite its perfection in his eyes. He made a mental note to work on that, too.

"You will not move out of your position," he said, "no matter what I do to you. You don't need to remain silent, not for this particular exercise, but you do need to remain still. Are we quite clear on this, Shea?"

"Yes, sir," she whispered.

Ah, *sir* again. Yes, the girl was a natural.

Liam started slowly. He ran his finger down her cheek. She stayed still, save for a slight shiver as he drew his finger along her throat and over her collarbone. Playing on this reaction, he curled one hand lightly around her throat, just below the jaw line, and applied the lightest of pressure.

"Oh!" she cried, her breath now coming more rapidly. After a moment, he released his hold. She drew in a deep, shuddering breath.

"You're doing great," Liam murmured, pleased with her sensitivity, and with her ability to stay in position in the face of what clearly had been a trigger. Stepping back a little, he reached for her breasts, which he cupped and lifted, loving the solid heft of those perfect, round globes. He squeezed gently, and then a little harder, again pulling another gasp from her strawberry lips. He flicked at her erect nipples and grasped them between forefinger and thumb, tugging gently. She moaned.

Liam wanted nothing more than to throw her down then and there and fuck her again. He let go of her nipples and took a step back. Now was not the time to give in to his own impulses. While making love to her had been sublime, if he was going to give Shea the training he believed she needed and longed for, he had to keep his own base impulses under better control, especially when they were in the dungeon.

As much to distract himself as anything, Liam turned away. He went to the toy wardrobe. Opening the doors, he selected an item and returned to Shea, pleased to see she was still holding her position. Removing the plastic wrapper, he held it up for Shea to see. "This is a collar." He fingered the stiff black leather. "I like to use these in training for two reasons. First, they're handy." He rang a finger along one of the large metal rings embedded at intervals along the leather. "The D rings make for quick, easy tethering. And then there's the erotic aspect. Lift your hair from your neck and I'll show you."

Shea didn't react right away. "Go on," Liam urged. "Do as you're told."

Biting her lower lip, Shea reached for her shoulder-length hair and twisted it into a ponytail with her fingers. Liam could see how nervous she was, but at the same time her lovely nipples were jutting toward him like little headlights. His mouth watered with the desire to taste them once more, and he swallowed hard.

Moving behind her, he buckled the collar around her neck, leaving it loose, but not too loose. Bending close, he murmured in her ear, "The collar symbolizes possession. For some, to be collared is to be owned. It represents your surrender of control, your willingness to submit."

Her shapely ass was grazing his thighs and if he hadn't been wearing shorts his cock would have sprung forward in full erection. Unable to help himself, he kissed the nape of her neck, his lips caressing the soft skin. Shea offered a sound somewhere between a moan and a sigh.

Catching himself, Liam stepped back. Again he cleared his throat. "You may drop your arms," he said brusquely. "We'll start the first exercise on the spanking bench." He led the naked, collared girl to the bench. "I'll need you to lean your torso over the bench so that your body is resting along the length of the top bar. Let your arms hang down and position your legs on either side so your ass is sticking out." He bent over the bench himself in a quick demonstration. Shea was watching with the deer-in-the-headlights look she'd offered the night before, though now he knew she wasn't acting.

He stood and turned toward her. "I'm not going to cuff you to the bench at this point. That will come later, when you're ready to handle more intensity."

He guided her over the top of the bench, pleased to note the height was just about perfect to allow her to extend her body along it while keeping her feet flat on the floor. As he helped her into position, he could feel her trembling. Crouching beside her, he placed his hand lightly on her back as he looked into her face. "Shea, are you okay? You're so quiet. You're allowed to talk, you know. It helps me to understand what's going on with you right now."

"I'm nervous," she admitted, again biting her lower lip. "I mean, this is so weird. I can't believe I'm even doing this!"

"We can stop any —"

"No," she interrupted. "I don't want to stop. I'm just scared, but I can work through it. I need to figure this stuff out. I need to understand why I broke down the way I did, and why I had such a—why last night when you spanked me I—" She blew out a breath, not completing the thought that clearly caused her embarrassment.

Liam's heart ached with tenderness. He stroked the hair from Shea's face, tucking it behind her ear. "I understand, Shea. I do. You don't have to give voice to things that embarrass you, but I want you to understand that what you experienced last night is natural and beautiful. And your powerful, sensual reaction was exactly what I would expect of a true submissive." He ran his hand lightly over her bare back, pleased as he felt her relax.

Leaning down, he opened the toy box that was set near the bench and extracted a short-handled riding crop that was dyed a rich burgundy red. He smacked the folded leather end against his thigh. Shea whipped her head toward the cracking sound, her lips parting into an O, her hands curling into fists.

"That's right," Liam said, feeling his power expand like light inside his chest. "It's time to explore your penchant for erotic pain."

Chapter 7

She looked both exquisitely lovely and exquisitely vulnerable, and Liam couldn't decide which excited him more. She lay stretched facedown along the top bar of the spanking bench, her head turned to the side so her cheek rested against the padded leather. Her breasts bulged like plump, ripe melons beneath her. Her legs were spread on either side of the bench to expose the sweet pooch of her pussy beneath her voluptuous ass.

"We'll start out slowly," Liam informed the lovely girl. "I'm just going to warm the skin first and let you get used to the feel of the leather. Okay, Shea?"

She gave a slight nod.

Time to add a bit of protocol.

"Shea, when your trainer asks you a direct question, you will respond with a direct, audible answer. I need more than a nod so I can be sure you understand what's being asked of you, especially as we get deeper into the training process. So, let's try it again. Are you ready for me to start the cropping?"

Shea blew out a breath. "Yes, sir," she finally said. "I'm ready."

Liam, behind her and thus out of her line of vision, permitted himself a smile. "You sound like you're being sent to the gallows or something."

There was a long pause, and then she said, "I'm scared. I want it—I think. I'm just scared."

Liam set down the crop and moved from behind her to stand beside her. "I understand. This can be scary stuff we're exploring. But good stuff, too. I promise." He stroked her back. He could feel the tension in her body. Reaching for her shoulders, he kneaded her rigid muscles until he felt her relax, if just a little.

"Remember," he said, "this isn't about inflicting pain. It's about sensation, and where that sensation leads you, if you let it. You ready to try it?"

Shea nodded, though she still looked nervous as a cat.

"What was that?" he asked gently.

"Yes, sir" she whispered, finally smiling.

He smiled back and kissed her cheek.

Moving again behind her, he retrieved the crop and dragged the leather thong slowly over her back. She shuddered at its touch. He moved down to her ass and lifted the crop, letting the thong fall lightly on one cheek and then the other, just a tap. Shea tensed, her hands curling into fists.

"Relax your body and your hands, Shea," Liam said. "Try not to tense your muscles. Don't wriggle around, or the crop might land where it's not intended. Okay?"

"Yes. Okay."

Liam began to smack her ass and thighs with a light but steady stroke. Her fingers slowly unfurled as he warmed her skin. Liam, who had in-depth personal experience of every BDSM toy he ever used on a sub, knew that the sensation of the soft leather stroking and warming the skin was at first quite pleasurable. It could lull you in the same way a good massage could, with its steady tap-tap-tap to quicken blood flow and awaken nerve endings.

Once he determined Shea was sufficiently relaxed and ready, he moved to the next level with the first real stinging blow, delivered to her left ass cheek. Predictably, Shea squealed as she twisted back to cast an accusing glare.

Liam bit back his smile. "Remain in position, Shea."

"That hurt," she whined.

"It was supposed to. Turn around, face forward. We're just getting started."

He waited a beat, and then two, in case she decided to call it quits. If she did, he wouldn't cajole or press her to continue. At this point they were still in the experiment stage. Based on his assessment of her reactions the night before and during their subsequent conversations, he believed she was in fact sexually submissive and masochistic, but what he believed didn't really matter, not if she wasn't willing to explore the possibilities. Submission had to be fully consensual, the exchange of power mutual, or he wasn't interested.

She drew in a breath and slowly returned to her position, resting her cheek once more on the padded leather and closing her eyes. Liam refused to linger on the small bubble of exultance rising inside him, as his more rational mind tamped down his excitement. He'd known Shea only a little over twenty-four hours. He wasn't yet ready to admit how much this mattered to him. Whatever he thought he was feeling could only be infatuation. There was no such thing as love at first sight.

Liam closed his eyes a moment, steadying himself to focus on the task at hand. He resumed the cropping, delivering a series of rapid stinging blows to the jiggling, fleshy globes of her ass until the skin turned pink.

Shea was panting. "Slow your breathing," Liam said in a soothing tone. "Easy, deep breaths. That's it. In…and out. In…and out." He waited, watching as she tried to comply.

"Better," he said. "I'm going to increase the intensity now. I know you can handle this," he added, thinking back to the quite hard spanking he'd delivered the night before. "Just relax into the pain. Embrace the sting." Again, he waited a beat in case she balked. She remained still, though her hands were once more balled into fists.

The red leather thong slapped against the backs of her thighs with a satisfying smacking sound that was punctuated by her sweet gasps and whimpers. Liam knew it stung quite a bit more on those slender thighs than on her lush bottom, and he adjusted the intensity accordingly, though he still hit her hard enough to turn the skin a lovely shade of dark pink.

When her thighs were nearly as pink as her ass, and Shea was whimpering steadily, Liam reached between her legs with his free hand and stroked along her labia. He was delighted, though not really surprised, to find that she was sopping wet. She moaned as he pressed a finger into the hot, tight clutch of her cunt, and actually wriggled back against him. Had she been fully trained, he would have punished her for behaving like a wanton slut, instead of an obedient slave girl. His cock, however, fully approved of the behavior, straining against his shorts in a show of appreciation.

Liam ran his now-slick finger in a light circle over the hard nubbin of her clit and she moaned again. "Pleasure," he said, this time pressing two fingers into her wet heat, "can be greatly heightened by erotic pain." While keeping one hand at her sex, he struck her ass with the crop hard enough to leave its imprint, a dark red rectangle against the already-pink skin. Shea jerked and cried out, her vaginal muscles spasming against his fingers.

"Stay still," Liam ordered. He struck her again, adding a second rectangular mark on the other ass cheek. Her clit was like a swelling pea beneath his fingertips as he continued to stroke and tease her sex. Each moan of pleasure was followed by a shriek of pain as Liam struck her ass and thighs again and again with the crop.

"Pleasure, pain, pleasure, pain," he murmured as he continued with the intentional overload of sensation brought about by the sharp, steady sting of the crop juxtaposed with the sensual pleasure of his hand at her sex. Shea began to tremble uncontrollably, her hands clenched tight, her head whipping in a frenzy of dark shiny hair from side to side over the bench, her ass twitching with each stinging blow as she pressed back against his hand.

"I can't, I can't, I can't, oh, oh, oh, oh god, no, help me, please, I can't…" she chanted over and over in a breathless, desperate prayer.

"You can," he urged. "You are."

Liam wanted nothing more than to drop the crop, tear off his shorts and plunge his cock into the girl, but he held himself back. This wasn't about him. This was about Shea, and he owed it to her as her trainer to bring the exercise, along with the girl, to a satisfying climax.

Her breathy pleas deepened into a kind of feral moan as several deep shudders wracked her already trembling form. Liam didn't let up, continuing to smack and to tease her until the shudders subsided and she lay as limp as a ragdoll against the bench, her face obscured by the tumult of her hair.

Liam dropped the crop and moved to stand beside her, placing his hand lightly on the small of her back. "Hey," he said softly.

Shea didn't respond.

"Hey, you. You alive? You okay?"

He expected her to lift her head then, or at least reply. Instead, she made a small sobbing sound, and her shoulders began to shake. It took Liam a few seconds to realize she was crying. Watching her, his heart cracked with tenderness.

"Shea, Shea, honey, what is it? Hey, it's okay." He reached beneath her and lifted her into his arms. He carried her to the daybed and laid her gently on the mattress. She turned toward the wall and curled into a fetal ball, still sobbing.

Liam sat beside her and stroked her back, crooning softly, "It's okay, baby. It's all good. Just let it go. Let it out. That's it, baby, that's it." Finally he lay down beside her and wrapped his body around hers, holding her shaking form until she slowly relaxed against him.

They lay together for a long time. Shea had quieted, her breathing now deep and even. Liam wondered if she'd fallen asleep. For himself, he would have been content to lie there forever, just holding the sweet girl and feeling the warmth of her body against his.

Man, oh, man, you've got it bad, Jordan.

Yes, he was falling, and falling hard, for this woman. He wanted to comfort her, to ravish her, to claim her. While his mind coolly informed him that he barely knew her, his body and more importantly, his heart, told him he knew her in all the ways that truly mattered, and had always known her.

"Hopeless romantic," he murmured before realizing he had spoken aloud.

Apparently not asleep after all, Shea twisted around to stare at him with her tear-stained face. "What?" she croaked, and then, before he could reply, "You hate me, right? I'm just a mess. I fucked up again."

Liam laughed. "Are you nuts? Didn't you pay attention to anything we talked about before? Crying is *not* a negative thing, Shea. Crying is a release, and clearly you have a lot to let go of."

Shea pulled out of his arms and sat up, wrapping her arms protectively around her torso. "Crying is a sign of weakness."

Liam shook his head. "I don't know where you got that idea. Crying is a sign of strength. A sign you're connecting on a deeply intimate level to what's going on here. I'm proud of you, Shea. You didn't fuck up. You were fantastic. You're amazing. Spectacular. I can't wait to take you further into the process. I've rarely seen such a natural, pure bent toward sensual submission. You were born for this, Shea."

And I was born for you.

~*~

Shea stood in the awkward at-attention pose, her arms behind her back. She would have been content to just lie in the narrow bed, safe in Liam's arms forever, but after a while he had asked if she was ready for the next lesson and she had said she was, though in fact she doubted she could tolerate another experience as intense as the one she'd just endured.

The session on the spanking bench had been nothing short of astounding. At first she'd just been focused on the stinging blows of the crop. She'd gritted her teeth, determined to get through it, to show Liam she was as strong as he seemed to think she was.

Then, when he'd started touching her pussy, oh! In spite of the cropping, or perhaps because of it, she hadn't realized how deeply aroused she was. The cropping had hurt, make no mistake, the building pain of the relentless stroke of stinging leather on increasingly tender skin almost too much to bear. The odd thing was, it hadn't hurt any less once he began to rub and tease her engorged cunt, if anything it hurt *more*, in contrast to the blinding pleasure of his erotic touch.

But that hadn't mattered. Or more precisely, it was the blending of the two sensations, the pleasure and the pain, twisting together into braided tendrils of pure, intense sensation that surpassed anything she'd ever experienced in her life. The orgasm that had thundered through her was even more powerful than the one he'd pulled from her the night before. She'd felt as if she were at once dying and being reborn. She wanted it to stop, oh, to stop, and at the same time to never, ever end.

Then came the tears.

Again.

The flood of quaking, explosive sobbing that swept her along in its wake, leaving her powerless, utterly exposed and completely undone.

At the same time, she had luxuriated in Liam's tender embrace as he crooned his sweet reassurances that it was okay to cry. She even believed him on an intellectual level. But something deep inside, a persistent pervasive shame at her weakness, continued to eat away at her.

Shea Annette Devon simply did not cry.

She wouldn't cry again. She would be a good student and pay attention to the lessons her trainer wanted her to learn. She took a deep breath and lifted her chin as Liam outlined his expectations for the next lesson.

"You've proven yourself a natural when it comes to erotic suffering and masochistic pleasure. Now I'd like pick up where we left off earlier this morning. I want to test more fully your ability to submit with grace to things you might find uncomfortable. We got a little sidetracked earlier."

Shea snorted at the memory of her repeated breakdowns. Was she going to cry every fucking time things got a little intense? She lifted her chin higher, determined to hold it together this time, no matter what.

Liam smiled and reached out to touch her chin. "Relax," he said. "You're not a soldier. I want you to stand with an easy grace, breasts thrust out proud, legs firmly planted shoulder-width apart, your head at a natural angle, eyes on the floor to signify respect."

Shea jerked her head up at this. *Eyes on the floor? Respect? What the hell?*

To her chagrin, Liam actually laughed. "Shea, this training isn't just about giving you mind-blowing orgasms"—Shea felt herself color at this pronouncement—"it's also about learning submission and obedience. I'm not here to teach you to be a masochistic slut"—Liam grinned—"not that you need any teaching in that regard." Shea felt the heat in her face intensify.

Liam put his hand on her shoulder, and his eyes were kind as he added, "Seriously, Shea. It's also about surrender, in the best sense of the word. It's about letting go of the rigid control you feel you have to maintain at all times. It's about accepting that someone else is going to be making the decisions for a while. Someone else is going to care for you, but they are also going to dictate what you do, when you do it and how you do it. It's part and parcel of submissive training, along with the whippings and the orgasms." He dropped his hand and stepped back. "At least it is when I'm the trainer."

Easy for you to say. You're not the one standing here butt naked waiting for god knows what to happen.

Stop it. Trust him. You can trust him.

"Okay," Shea said aloud. "I think I know what you're saying, though I probably should have done a little more research into this whole thing before I jumped in with both feet." She blew out a determined breath. "But okay. Let's do this thing."

Again Liam smiled, shaking his head slightly. Shea silently cursed herself. She had to stop approaching this like a business deal she was structuring. She needed to — what was it he'd said — to let go.

"The first thing I'm going to do," Liam said, as he walked in a slow circle around her, "is inspect your body."

Shea twisted her head to follow his path. Liam shook his head and said sharply, "Back in position! Maintain an at-attention stance until I tell you to move."

Shea had to bite back the retort that no one told her what to do. This was just an exercise, she reminded herself. Liam knew what he was doing. She turned back and looked obediently at the floor, though it made her uncomfortable to have him out of her line of vision and, no doubt, staring at her big ass.

Finally he returned to stand in front of her. Shea resisted the urge to look up into his face, remembering the admonition to keep her eyes down. "Put your hands behind your head," he ordered. "Lace your fingers behind your neck."

Shea did look up then, staring directly into Liam's eyes for a moment. She was disconcerted by the power she saw there, and the determination. There was no trace of the tenderness there'd been when he'd talked so sweetly to her as they lay together on the daybed. The lover, she supposed, was on break. The trainer had taken his place.

Taking a breath, she did as she was told. As she reached beneath her hair, she was startled to feel the metal buckle of the leather collar he'd placed around her neck before the bench session. It was loose around her throat, and somehow she'd almost forgotten it was there. The whole concept of a collar, a *slave* collar, seemed both alien and, if she were completely honest, exciting to her. It conveyed images of perfumed harem girls in swirling silks with ankle bracelets made from tiny golden bells that tinkled as they danced seductively for their Masters.

Liam traced a circle around her nipples, which at once perked to immediate attention. He cupped her breasts, lifting and letting them fall. He ran his hands down her sides and briefly cupped her sex. It took every ounce of self-control not to lean into his touch. Had she ever wanted anyone as much as she wanted this man?

"Now," Liam continued, "bend over and reach for your ankles. Keep your legs spread wide while I inspect your ass."

His words hit her like a blow. Shea didn't move. Standing there naked with her hands behind her head was one thing. Bending over so he could inspect her ass was quite another!

Shea liked her body overall. Her breasts were a perky 34C and gravity hadn't yet done any damage. Her waist was long and slender, as were her legs. But her ass was another matter. It was, to put it bluntly, too big for the rest of her. She'd always been sensitive about it, and had been careful to dress in a way that minimized that particular part of her anatomy.

Now the thought of Liam focusing on it, not just for the purpose of spanking or cropping her, but expressly to "inspect" it, was too much, despite her recent promise to herself to obey him.

"Shea," Liam said in a warning tone, "are you refusing me?"

Fuck.

Why was this so hard?

He's already seen more of your ass than anyone else ever has. Stop being an idiot.

Shea dropped her arms and bent forward, awkwardly reaching for her ankles, which was difficult while still keeping her legs spread. She was glad Liam couldn't see her face, as she was certain she was blushing, yet again. She had never blushed so much in her life as she had in the space of a day and a half with this man.

"You've got a few marks that will stick around for a day or two," he commented as he ran his fingers sensually over her ass and thighs. "You should be proud, Shea. You took quite a cropping. Like I said before, you're definitely a natural."

Shea smiled at this, feeling ridiculously pleased at his praise. The smile fell away as he said, "Now, reach back and spread your ass cheeks for me, and hold that position."

Christ. Was he serious?

Shea bit her lip. She'd had boyfriends who were overly-interested in her ass, but those relationships had never lasted long. Shea had zero interest in anal sex, and she certainly wasn't comfortable with someone staring at her asshole, thank you!

"Shea." Again the warning tone.

With a sigh she couldn't suppress, Shea reluctantly brought her hands behind her and reached for her ass cheeks. Tentatively she placed her fingers on her bottom, willing herself to do as he commanded.

Commanded!

What the hell was she doing?

Yes, she had wanted to explore her strong reaction to the fusion of pleasure and what he termed erotic pain, but this was something else again. She hadn't signed up to be humiliated. She let her hands fall to her sides.

"I can't," she said.

"Of course you can," Liam countered.

"No. I can't."

"You mean you won't?"

Shea stood slowly and turned to face him. "I guess so."

"All right, then." Liam shrugged and she could have sworn he was suppressing a grin. "You'll just have to be punished."

Chapter 8

Liam flicked the channels with the remote, though he had no idea what was on the screen. He was watching Shea instead, which was much more interesting than anything that might be on TV.

Why was it women so often zoned in on one part of their body and decided it was flawed? Especially when it was the very feature that lifted them from merely attractive to devastatingly sexy? So it was with Shea Devon. That voluptuous ass of hers was perfect in every way. Perfect for spanking, for whipping, for fucking...

Poor thing—he almost felt sorry for her, positioned as she was on the wide, low coffee table with her bare ass splayed for his viewing pleasure. She was kneeling face down, her arms cradling her head, her knees spread wide. She could have refused the punishment. She could have called the whole thing off. Instead, she'd lowered her head and nodded, and he could sense the relief in her gesture. She wanted to be taken in hand—she longed to surrender.

Sitting on the sofa behind her, he had a full view of her puckered pink asshole and the delicate curve of her labia. He knew if he could have seen her face he would see the flush of embarrassment there. He'd seen the flash of barely suppressed outrage when he'd informed her of the precise nature of her punishment.

She had no doubt been expecting something more traditional, such as a spanking, but for people like her, a spanking wouldn't have been a punishment, unless he delivered one so blistering it left her with bruises. She certainly wasn't ready for that sort of punishment, nor would it have been appropriate, given the mild nature of her misdeed. No, it was better to address her excessive modesty with a forced display. Over time, if he did his job right, the very thing that now caused her such embarrassment would become a source of pride.

He glanced at the time. Ten minutes was long enough for this punishment, and it had probably seemed a lot longer to the naked girl. Clicking off the remote, he leaned forward and reached for her. At his touch, she stiffened, though she stayed in position. "I'm going to examine your ass now," Liam said. "I want you to stay as still as you can during the process. If you move or resist, we'll just have to start over. Okay, Shea?"

"Yes, sir," came the muffled reply. Liam allowed himself to smile. Christ, she was so fucking cute and sexy it hurt. It was hard to believe she hadn't signed up for the BDSM packet. She was such a natural.

Forcing himself to remain professional, Liam said, "Modesty has no place in a D/s relationship." He let his finger trail along the cleft between her ass cheeks. Shea's inhalation of breath was audible, but still she kept her position. Good girl. He reached for the tube of lubricant he'd set beside her on the coffee table. Flipping open the cap, he squeezed a small amount onto his index finger and then touched the tip of his finger to her asshole. Shea shuddered at his touch.

Liam ran his finger in a light circle over and around the pucker as Shea twitched in her effort to remain still. "Sometimes submission is hard. Like anything worth having, it takes work and commitment. And trust. A trainer will look for a trigger—something about which you are especially sensitive, something he can use to help you break down the walls that are going to prevent you from truly letting go. Your job is to submit. It's really that simple. If you can trust that I am helping you get to where you need to go, you don't have to think through all the angles or debate with yourself about the pros and cons. You just do it. You take it. You submit. Do you understand?"

"I don't know." Shea's voice was low and seductively sultry.

Liam wanted to drape his body over hers and bury his face in her neck. Instead, he said, "Okay. That's honest. And it's okay not to know. Again, that's where trust comes in." He continued to rim her asshole with his finger while stroking her back with his other hand. He was pleased to feel some of the tension draining from her body.

"I'm going to work with you on your aversion to someone looking at and touching your ass. If you are truly to submit, you must give of yourself completely. That means that, during the training, every part of your body belongs to me. Even your ass." He pushed his lubed fingertip carefully past her sphincter, feeling its tight clutch at his first knuckle. His cock throbbed and he blew out a breath to stay focused.

Shea jerked sharply so that his finger fell away. Though she remained on her hands and knees on the table, she twisted around to stare defiantly at him. "I don't do anal sex," she announced in a tone that brooked no argument

Back in full trainer mode, Liam reached for a tissue and wiped his lubricated finger, taking his time and keeping his expression impassive. Shea continued to stare at him, the challenge clear in her expression.

Liam stood and pulled Shea up from the table, lifting her to her feet. He spun her toward him and gripped her shoulders as he looked down into her face. "When you are being trained by me, Shea, you do what I tell you to do." He stared down at her, daring her to contradict him.

A play of emotions moved over Shea's face like a storm, her eyes flashing. Liam moved one hand from her shoulder to her throat, letting his fingers graze the flesh above the collar in a show of pure dominance as he continued to stare down at her. Mentally he was rooting for her, willing her not to balk, not to back away from what he knew she craved, if she could just get out of her own way.

He let his fingers curl lightly around her neck, pressing the tips of his thumb and index finger against the soft skin just beneath her jaw line. "For this week, your body and your will belong to me. I call the shots. I make the rules. You will follow them. Is that clearly understood?"

They continued to lock eyes. Was this it? Had he pushed her too far, too fast? Despite her resistance, he could still feel the underlying longing emanating from a place deep inside her. She needed this. The question was, did she have the courage to accept it?

He kept his hand on her throat, waiting.

Relief flooded through him as her expression finally softened, her lips parting. "Yes," she breathed. "Yes, sir."

~*~

Shea was lying on the apparatus Liam called the pivot table, which reminded her of a combination of a gynecological exam table and a dentist's chair, except for the leg and armrests with leather cuffs designed to hold a person spread eagle. Liam had positioned Shea on her back on the padded leather, legs spread wide in the restraints, her pussy and ass fully exposed and on display on the edge of the seat.

The odd thing was, she had been fully prepared to tell Liam to go to hell after his declaration that her body and her will belonged to him. Exploring submissive and masochistic impulses was one thing — giving herself body and soul to a man she barely knew was quite another!

And yet…

Raw masculine power and sensuality had radiated from him as he'd gripped her throat. She'd actually felt as if she were melting beneath his gaze and his dominant touch, both her body and her will. She'd barely been able to suppress the moan of pure, animal lust that had risen in her throat as he had stared down at her.

She hadn't uttered a word of protest as he led her by the hand back to the dungeon and directed her to lie down on the pivot table. She'd watched in mute acceptance as he cuffed her wrists, thighs and ankles in place. Now she stared with wide eyes as he held up a black rubber phallus the thickness of a large finger, its base flaring and then narrowing again.

Liam stripped off the plastic wrapper. "This is an anal plug. It's the smallest size, and a good place for us to start."

Shea swallowed hard and tried to close her legs. She couldn't budge an inch. She fought down a sudden surge of panic. "I don't think I like the look of that."

Liam nodded. "I don't imagine you do. Yet." He squirted some lubricant from a tube and spread it over the head of the plug. Crouching in front of her, he placed one hand on her inner thigh. She could feel his warm breath on her skin. In spite of her predicament and her fear, the spark of lust he'd engendered earlier with his primal touch fanned into flames inside her.

"Sometimes," Liam said as he touched the gooey tip of the phallus to her asshole, "the very thing we resist so much is also the thing we need. The only thing standing between you and true submission is fear." The push was gentle but inexorable against the ring of muscle guarding this most private of passages. "I will help you move past the fear, if you'll let me. Together we'll strip away that cloak of modesty you've wrapped around yourself. He pressed harder, and Shea felt the phallus slip deeper inside her. She gripped the armrests with her fingers.

"Relax," Liam urged. "It'll be much easier if you can relax, I promise. And more than that, it's a sign you're letting go. It shows me you're working with me, rather than fighting me on this." He pushed the plug deeper, pulling another gasp from Shea's lips. "Because it's going to happen, Shea, whether you work with me or against me." He pushed the plug the rest of the way, and as the widening base of the thing slipped inside her, Shea felt a sudden sharp pain shoot through her anus.

"Ow!" she cried, "that hurts!"

Liam nodded as he stood. "It would have hurt less if you were relaxed. We'll work on that." He patted her thigh and smiled. "It's in. Your first anal plug. You should be proud."

Shea tried to summon the appropriate outrage at this declaration, but realized with no small surprise that she was, in fact, proud. She'd always told the guys she'd dated who were interested in anal sex that she was especially sensitive in that area. She'd said it so often that she had come to believe it herself. Yet here she lay with a butt plug up her ass and it was fine! Well, maybe not exactly fine. It was humiliating, but at least it didn't hurt, not now that it was in. It felt kind of snug, that was all. Okay, it was more than that. It felt kind of…sexy. How weird was that?

"Want to see?" Liam's question shook her out of her reverie.

"No!" Shea said at once, the response a reflex. But then she thought about it. Did she want to see? She was kind of curious what it must look like. After all, he had the advantage right now, because he could see it and she couldn't. "I mean, yes," she amended. "I think."

Liam brought over a large freestanding mirror and placed it in front of Shea. At first she closed her eyes, embarrassed at the image of herself cuffed and spread eagle, her pussy and ass on full display. But curiosity won out, and she opened her eyes. All that showed of the plug was a flat circle of flexible plastic covering her asshole between her ample cheeks. She stared, fascinated at the way her labia had swelled and spread like the petals of a flower above the offending plug. She couldn't remember the last time she'd really examined her own naked body, certainly not in this sort of intimate way. Her spread labia glistened and she tried to tell herself it was just the lubricant from the plug, but she knew better. In fact, her clit was throbbing. If her hands had been free, she might not have been able to resist the temptation to rub herself, just a little, to ease the ache.

"Sexy, huh?"

Shea startled at the sound of Liam's deep voice. He was standing just behind her, out of her line of sight, and for a second, she'd almost forgotten he was there. "Oh! I...I don't know."

"Yes, you do," Liam contradicted, as if he could read her mind. "It *is* sexy, and I'm not just talking about how hot you look in that position. Nothing is sexier for people like you and me than true submission." He lifted a tendril of hair that had fallen into her face and tucked it behind her ear. Unable to stop herself, she leaned into his hand. She wanted to kiss his fingers and only just stopped herself in time.

Liam stepped away and moved the mirror from between her legs. "Punishment is over, and we move on now with a clean slate." Crouching in front of her, he tugged gently at the plug and it slid out. Again Shea experienced a strong impulse to close her legs, but of course, she could not. She watched as Liam dropped the plug into a bowl and silently prayed there was nothing on it but lube. Just the thought made her cringe with embarrassment and she closed her eyes.

She heard Liam moving about the room, and then felt his presence when he crouched once more between her legs. "You did so well with the starter plug that I think we'll move right on to this one."

Shea's eyes flew open at these words. "What?" she blurted. Liam was holding up a considerably thicker plug, perhaps three fingers wide. "You said punishment was over!"

Liam nodded. "It is. This is just training. You did so well with that, we're moving forward."

Shea shook her head vigorously. "No. No way."

"Shea." Liam's voice was calm but firm. "Please don't let your fear control your responses. You don't want another punishment, surely?" Shea pressed her lips together, not trusting herself to reply. Liam continued, "I wouldn't suggest this if I wasn't fully confident you could handle it. If you relax, you'll barely notice it once it's in."

"Ha," she retorted, unable to help herself. "That's easy for you to say. You're the one sticking it in. I bet you'd have a hard time having that thing shoved up your ass."

Liam's lips twitched into a smile. "In point of fact, the anus can accommodate quite a bit more than this little thing. The largest anal plugs are as wide around as a soda bottle at their base, and they're all safe for insertion, when it's done correctly."

"A soda bottle?" Shea echoed faintly.

Liam shook his head. "Don't worry. I have no intention of using one of those on you. There is a plug one size larger than this that we might try at some point, if you wish. But for the purpose of our initial training, this is as far as we'll go." He squeezed a dollop of lubricant over the hard, black rubber. "Oh, and to answer your question, I do remember the first time, Shea. It was a little, shall we say, unnerving. But no, it really wasn't that hard."

Shea lifted her eyebrows in surprise. "You—you let someone do this to you?"

Liam nodded. "I did. I would never do anything to you that I hadn't experienced firsthand." He let this sink in a moment and then said, "Now, are you ready to continue, Shea? I know you can do this. Show me how strong you are—how brave."

Shea, who had opened her mouth to protest again, shut it. She *was* strong and brave. She could do this. Liam was sure she could. She just needed to relax. She needed to trust him. She nodded her head slowly and closed her eyes.

"Good girl," Liam said softly, and for some reason this bit of praise warmed Shea from the inside out.

She expected this wider plug to hurt more but, either because she was more relaxed, or because the first one had stretched her a little, or due to a combination of both things, this plug slipped in more easily than the first. Except for the last painful push as the flared base slid inside her. "Ow!" she squealed again, but then it was done.

"Excellent," Liam pronounced. He tapped the round end that protruded between her ass cheeks with his fingers. "You took that very well. I think a reward is in order."

Shea smiled again, waiting expectantly for him to pull the offending plug from her bottom and let her up from the pivot table. Instead, he walked toward the toy cabinet, this time returning with a long white wand with a large rubber ball at its end and a long cord protruding from its base. He inserted the electrical plug into a wall socket and came to stand once more between her legs.

He held up the wand. "Have you ever used one of these?"

Mutely, Shea shook her head.

"It's called a magic wand. It's sold as a massager, but I find it has much better uses than on sore muscles. It can provide a very powerful orgasm."

Shea swallowed hard, nervous but intrigued. "You don't, um, insert that thing, do you?"

Liam smiled and shook his head. "No, no. It's for external use only." Once again he picked up the tube of lubricant and squeezed some over the head of the vibrator. Crouching again between her legs, he touched the head, which was surprisingly soft, to her labia. "This is your reward, Shea. I want you to focus on the fullness in your ass while I use this on you." He flicked a switch on the side of the wand and it buzzed into vibrating life, at once sending tremors of sensation through Shea's loins. "You're going to come for me."

He moved the ball in a gentle circle, stimulating every nerve ending in Shea's throbbing pussy. She could already tell she was going to come fast with this thing, and wondered how she'd made it through her life as a single woman without discovering such a handy toy. It felt better than any hand-held device had a right to.

"One more thing," Liam said over the soft buzzing sound of the vibrator. "You won't come until I tell you to. That orgasm belongs to me."

What the fuck?

Shea tried but failed to muster her argument about the inability to control at will when one did or didn't orgasm. The wand was doing its magic, that was for sure, but in the process it seemed to be short-circuiting her ability to form or hold onto any coherent thought. She could feel the phallus vibrating deep inside her ass as the wand moved over her engorging labia. As odd as the realization was, the plug buried inside her seemed to be intensifying her pleasure, rather than detracting from it.

Within a few minutes, an impending orgasm rose inside her. "Oh god," she gasped. "I'm going to come!"

"No, you're not." Liam's voice was firm. "Not yet. Push it back. Wait for permission."

Shea shot a helpless look at the man crouched between her legs. "How…" she managed to gasp, before another wave of sensation hurtled through her.

"Look at me," Liam said. He was gazing deep into her eyes and, unable to help herself, she stared back. "Focus on my face and take your strength from me. Control your body. Do. Not. Come."

He moved the head of the wand over her clit and Shea began to tremble. Sweat broke over her skin and she couldn't seem to catch her breath. She stared into those deep, liquid brown eyes and somehow, she had no idea how, the desperate need to climax receded, just a little.

But then it rose again, cresting through her like a wave that was going to crash, no matter how hard she tried to keep it at bay. She wanted to obey him, but she had no idea how. "I can't—" she gasped.

"You did." Liam smiled. "Now come for me, beautiful girl. Come for me."

She let the wave crash over her, catching her in its tumult and toppling her into a swoon of pure, raw sensation so powerful she lost all sense of herself. When she finally opened her eyes, she realized she must have lost consciousness, however briefly.

Liam had released the cuffs that held her down and was lifting her into his arms. He carried her to the day bed and sank down onto it, still cradling her in his strong, warm embrace. She was dimly aware that the butt plug was still lodged inside her, but found that she didn't mind so much anymore. She nuzzled her head against Liam's chest and closed her eyes again, drifting in a place as peaceful as the sea outside the walls of the bungalow.

"I don't want this week to end," she surprised herself by saying, but she felt too relaxed to expend any energy denying it.

"It doesn't have to," Liam murmured back, so softly she might have only dreamed it.

Chapter 9

They sat side by side on a large beach blanket near the edge of the water. The ocean gleamed like black silk stippled with moonlight beneath the velvety sky.

They'd made dinner together, heating a delicious seafood casserole pulled from the fully stocked refrigerator, enjoying it with warm garlic bread and cold beer. By some silent agreement the talk during dinner had stayed on neutral topics, like Shea's career, the economy and how Houston had changed over the years they'd each been living there. As the meal progressed, Liam had felt Shea pulling back a little, putting some emotional distance between them. Or was he the one doing that?

"It's so beautiful out here," Shea said. "So peaceful. I almost feel guilty, like I should be doing something—checking my email, reading a prospectus, something! I honestly can't remember the last time I just sat still like this, gazing at the water, with no meetings to prepare for, no plans to keep."

"It's harder than it seems for someone like you, I'm guessing," Liam said, turning toward her. Her hair was blowing softly in the breeze, her face lifted slightly toward the sky. He wanted to kiss her long, slender throat, to reach for her, to pull her into his arms, but he didn't. He realized he wasn't quite sure where things stood between them. Were they lovers, or just trainer and sub girl? And what about when the week ended? What then?

Too soon to be asking these questions, he knew. Too soon even to be thinking them.

She faced him and shrugged. "Yeah. I guess it is. It's a tough business I'm in, even tougher because I'm a woman in a world still dominated by men. Even though Houston is a cosmopolitan city, it's still in Texas, and the business community is controlled by a fairly small group of rich old bastards who resent anyone trying to encroach on what they regard as their territory. I can't tell you how many times I've been confused for the secretary, called 'little lady', or asked to get the coffee."

"So you counter this by being smarter and working harder than anyone around you."

She smiled, her white teeth gleaming in the moonlight. "Exactly. I still do the makeup and wear the heels and keep my so-called feminist ideas to myself, but I've learned from some of the savviest women in the business. Bottom line, I structure the best deal for my client, and I don't take shit from any of these guys."

Liam laughed, imagining Shea Devon in a boardroom running rings around a bunch of fat, balding old men with no idea what had hit them. "I'm sure you don't."

Shea wrapped her arms around herself, her face closing. "That's why this whole sex slave thing doesn't sit right with me. It's not who I am."

Liam didn't say anything for a while as he pondered how to handle this sudden retreat, after the intensity of the day they'd shared. He knew now, with as much certainty as he'd ever known anything, that Shea was submissive in her core. Her responses to the training so far had been heartfelt and genuine. He could challenge her head-on, but he sensed that would result in more walls being raised. What was the root of her resistance?

Fear.

For whatever reason, Shea was afraid. It was up to Liam to make her feel safe.

"I agree," he said. "That's not who you are."

Shea whipped her head in his direction, affronted surprise on her face. "But you said before..." She paused, her eyebrows furrowing. "What about all that talk of my 'submissive potential'"—she made air quotes with her fingers—"and now you say that's not who I am? What, did I fail the training exercises?" Her tone was indignant. "I thought I did pretty good! I did everything you said, even when I didn't want to."

Liam laughed at the irony of her protest. "You did very well indeed, Shea. You exceeded all my expectations, if you want to know."

Shea looked at once mollified and confused. "So then, what? I don't get it. Why did you say that's not who I am?"

"As I recall," Liam retorted, unable to hide his grin, "You're the one who just said that."

Shea shook her head. "You know what I mean. Did you think I was faking?"

"Not at all. I agreed that you're not sex slave material. The training in which we're engaging is not sex slave training. It's just an exploration of your, as you've alluded to, submissive potential."

"There's a difference?"

Liam nodded. "Sure. A sex slave makes a one-time choice to submit and obey their Master in every aspect of their life. They opt to relinquish all rights to make decisions for themselves, and literally put their life into their Master's hands. It's a very special relationship, and I don't know too many people who really engage in that kind of lifestyle, 24/7, though they are out there.

"Unlike a slave," he continued, "a submissive renews the choice to submit at the beginning of each session with his or her Dom. The Dom and sub discover limits together, and they aren't necessarily static limits. For example, you might start out hating to be caned. I mean, really hating it, and fearing it. But as you develop in your masochistic exploration and as you come to realize and understand where a good caning can take you, you might come to love the intimate, searing stroke of the cane against your skin."

Shea shuddered. "A caning! No way. No way, José. Never."

Liam smiled. "Only last week, what would you have thought if someone said you'd have an incredibly powerful orgasm right after a blistering spanking?"

Though it was dark, Liam thought he could see the blush creeping over Shea's skin. "Well, that was a one-time—"

Liam interrupted, adding, "Or that you'd endure a cropping, and climax from that experience as well, not to mention taking two anal plugs and still managing another orgasm so intense you actually passed out from it."

Shea bit her lower lip, worrying it for a few seconds, before she finally said, "Okay. So maybe I'm sexually masochistic. That doesn't make me some kind of doormat."

"Absolutely not," Liam agreed emphatically. "Which isn't to say that the choice of sexual slavery makes one a doormat either. On the contrary, it takes a real strength to give up that measure of control. But I agree with what you said earlier—that's not who *you* are. Your focus, your need, lies more along the D/s part of the continuum. You long to submit to a strong Dom who understands your need to relinquish control. But at the heart of a D/s relationship is the ability to say *no* at any time. The focus is on the voluntary exchange of power."

He reached for one of her arms, still wrapped like armor around her body. She resisted at first, but then let him take her hand. He laced his fingers between hers and smiled at her. "It's like any intimate relationship—it takes work and open communication."

Shea shook her head. "All this talk of dominance and submission. You make it sound so—so *normal*."

Liam laughed. "To me it is. Not only normal, but natural and essential. It's the way I'm hardwired." He looked deep into her eyes, which sparkled with the reflection of the full moon over their heads. "It's the way you're hardwired, too, Shea, even if that's a scary thought for you."

Shea looked at him for a long time. Finally she said, "I'm not saying yes and I'm not saying no, but if I've learned anything so far, it's that I need to learn more." She pulled her hand away suddenly. "Wait a minute. You just said the heart of submission is the ability to say *no*. But earlier today you said the word *no* has no place in my vocabulary during the training."

Liam smiled again. "I'm glad you were paying attention. And yes, I did say that, or something close to it. But that's because you're in training. For this week, I suppose you could say it is more like a Master/slave relationship. Or you could think of it as submissive boot camp. It's a time of intensive training with very little negotiation. After all, it's not like we're in an actual relationship" — he paused, the last unspoken word balancing on his tongue. And then he let it fall from his lips as he reached once more for Shea's hand — "yet."

~*~

It shocked Shea to realize she had been teetering on the brink of a dark, negative place as Liam said those words — *it's not like we're in an actual relationship*. Of course, the more rational and controlled part of her mind understood and accepted that fact, but still the words ripped like barbed arrows through skin and bone and lodged painfully in her heart. Then he added that final word, and it was like a lifeline being tossed in the nick of time, and she reached for it, clutching it close.

She regarded him now, admiring his strong profile as he stared out at the water. She wanted to demand what precisely he meant by the word *yet*, and did he see them as continuing whatever it was they were exploring once they were both back in Houston?

Too soon, too soon, a voice inside her head warned, and she knew it was true. What was she even doing, thinking beyond this week? It wasn't as if she had time for a relationship back in the real world, and she suspected a D/s relationship would require even more of her time and energy than just having a boyfriend. It wouldn't be fair to Liam to lead him on. Her career came first.

Shea gave a small snort. What was her problem, anyway? She'd known the guy all of two days. Talk about jumping the gun. *Just stay in the moment,* she warned herself. *The future will take care of itself.* She glanced down at their hands, which were still entwined and lifted her gaze to see that Liam was smiling at her, his features silvered by the moon.

"I can't believe I just said that out loud." He gave a small laugh. "Very unprofessional of me to speak of relationships, I know. Forgive me if I overstepped."

"No, I...it's okay." More than okay, but Shea wasn't about to admit this. Already she cared way too much, and she knew it. Better to stay quiet and see where he was going with this.

"What I mean is," Liam continued, "I'm used to training subs. I'm used to helping them delve deep within themselves to find the grace and courage to submit. Without making too much of it, I believe it's a calling. That is, it's something that fulfills a need in me and, I hope, a need in them as well. But what I'm not used to..." He paused for a long time. Shea remained still, waiting.

Liam turned his face again toward the sea, and Shea could see he was marshalling his thoughts. Without turning back to her, he said, "I should tell you a little about me, Shea, so maybe you'll understand better." Liam blew out a breath. "You've heard the expression, the pot calling the kettle black?" He laughed, though there was no pleasure in it. "Remember this morning when I accused you of throwing yourself into your work as a way to avoid being disappointed in your personal life?"

"Yes," Shea said. Was it really only this morning? In some ways it was as if she'd known this man forever. How was that possible?

"Well, *I* do that, too. Though the process itself is deeply intimate by its very nature, I use D/s training as a way to keep people at arm's length. It's easy to demand honesty and courage from someone else, especially when you're the one in control. It's quite another to be honest and courageous yourself, especially when it comes to matters of the heart."

When was the last time a man had held her so in his thrall? She knew she should turn and run, as she always did when a man came too close for comfort, and yet she leaned toward him, eager, almost desperate, to hear what he had to say.

"Matters of the heart," she echoed.

Liam sighed. "To tell you the truth, Shea, I've been dishonest to some degree with you. What's been happening between us is about a lot more than just training, but I've been pretending otherwise because...because I was afraid."

Liam, the confident Master? Afraid? Shea was startled into saying, "Afraid of what?"

"The same thing you're afraid of. Intimacy."

Shea blinked at this. "What? Who said I was afraid of intimacy?"

"No one has to. It's evident in every aspect of your life."

Shea mulled this over, not liking this sweeping assessment, but unable to refute it.

Liam let go of her hand. "I'm trying to say I'm the same way, Shea." He drew his knees up to his chest and brought his arms around them, his expression suddenly brooding. "I'm thirty-three years old. I was married once in my twenties to a nice girl named Elizabeth. We were together for three years. We divorced on good terms, but, though I didn't realize it then, I never really knew her, nor did I ever really let her know me.

"Once I was on my own again, I began to explore my dominant impulses, and I came to understand my need for BDSM as a part of who I am. I've had a number of relationships with submissive women over the years, but they never lasted long. I always told myself I was holding out for that one woman with whom I could truly connect, but I realize now I never really gave anyone a chance. Though it wasn't a conscious decision, I used my role as Dom as a way to hold myself apart."

He turned to her. "Then you came along. I have to tell you, I never believed in love at first sight, but the moment I saw your picture, even before I met you, something deep inside me whispered, *she's the one.*" He lifted a hand as if to stop her from protesting. "I know, that's crazy, right? Especially after I realized you hadn't even signed on for the BDSM packet. I told myself, no way, she's not even into the lifestyle. Even then, Shea, even then, I was so taken with you I could hardly see straight."

He reached for her, cupping her cheek with his hand, his expression breathtakingly tender. "When we made love this afternoon, that was definitely *not* part of the script between trainer and sub. But even then I was trying to tell myself I was still just your trainer, and that I owed it to you as your trainer to keep myself aloof from my emotions."

He reached for one of the spaghetti straps of her sundress and pulled it slowly off her shoulder. Shea held her breath as he slipped his large hand into the top of her dress and cupped one of her breasts. She could feel her nipple perking to instant erection against his palm. Leaning toward her, he kissed her lips.

His mouth still on hers, Liam pushed her slowly down to the blanket and stretched out beside her, his hand still on her breast. The kiss moved from tender to urgent as Liam claimed her mouth with his lips and tongue. She could feel herself melting into a pool of liquid desire.

Finally, lifting his mouth from hers, Liam reached for the neckline of her dress. Shea gasped in startled surprise as he tore the fabric, ripping the dress open to reveal her naked body beneath it.

"Liam!" she cried, automatically trying to cover herself.

"I want you." In the light of the moon she could see that his pupils were dilated, his eyes hooded with lust. He began to kiss and bite her neck. "Not as a trainer, not as a Dom, but as a man."

He lifted himself over her. She could feel his hard cock beneath his shorts pressing against her. Her heart was fluttering like a captured bird in her chest, her breath rasping in her throat. "Please," she gasped, not sure what she was asking.

Somehow he got his shorts off and she could feel the insistent nudge of his cock between her legs. "You're mine." His mouth was close to her ear, his voice a guttural snarl of pure lust.

Fear and aching desire mingled into something so heady that Shea lost the capacity to think or speak. Beneath his solid masculine weight her cunt moistened, her legs parting of their own accord. When he plunged inside her, she was wet and ready, her vaginal muscles clamping down around his cock and pulling him in.

His strong hands pinned her wrists high over her head and he lowered his head once more to kiss her. Shea responded like a wild thing, panting and writhing beneath him, her hips arching up to take him as deep as he could go. Something in the way he moved inside her sent spirals of pleasure through her so fierce they could almost be called pain. It didn't matter, pleasure or pain, it was sublime.

"Fuck me! Fuck me! Oh, fuck, oh god!" Shea could hear the high-pitched wail that must be coming from her own lips, but she was powerless to stop the sound. Instead she gave in to it, and to the dominant man having his way with her, claiming her in that most primal of ways. He began to shudder as he continued to thrust, his groans wrenched from a place deep inside him. The orgasm he pulled from her seemed to go on and on, as if they were connected by an arc of electricity that held them both suspended in its lightning grip.

Finally they fell apart, both gasping for breath. As her pounding heart slowed, Shea became aware of the sound of the waves slapping in a hypnotic rhythm against the shore. She could feel the cool sand beneath the blanket and a sudden gust of salty air made her shiver.

Liam reached for her, pulling her into his strong, warm arms. "I think," he murmured, "I'm falling in love."

Oh, those magic, dangerous words. Words that, in Shea's experience, spelled the beginning of the end of a relationship. Even if she didn't consciously want to, she would start to withdraw once those fateful words were uttered, even if things were going great. Something she couldn't control inside herself would tell her it was time to pull back and shut any windows and doors that might have been accidentally opened in her heart.

Not this time.

Even if she'd wanted to shut those portals to her heart, to turn and run like the wind, for the first time in her life she was powerless in the face of whatever crazy emotions were careening through her.

"I think," she whispered back, stunned as the words tumbled from her mouth, "I am too."

Chapter 10

The sun was warm on Shea's bare back. Her arms were extended on either side, rope wound around her wrists and pulled taut, secured between two tall, thin palm trees. She was naked, her toes curling in the sand beneath her feet, her hair blowing in the gentle but constant sea breeze. Liam had promised he would be right back and of course she believed him, but that didn't stop her from fidgeting with anxious anticipation.

She could hear the sound of the delivery boat's engine. Liam had assured her this part of the island wasn't visible from the dock, but then he'd said, "Though, if I decide to let Scott admire my naked sub girl, that's my prerogative, isn't it, Shea?"

When he spoke like that, his voice deepening with authority, his dark, lovely eyes boring directly into her soul, Shea's mouth would go dry, any thought of refusal dying on her lips. This morning Shea's first impulse was to protest—no way was she going to let some stranger gawk at her—but her reply, spoken in a soft, submissive tone that came from somewhere deep inside her, was only, "Yes, Sir."

Since they'd made love on the sand, neither of them had uttered that fateful L word again, but something had clearly changed between them. Shea had stopped resisting her own impulses as she came to trust Liam more fully. She had stopped trying to define just what it was developing between them, and let herself go with the flow. This "letting go" was something entirely new for Shea. She was so used to keeping such tight control over every aspect of her life that, until now, she knew no other way to be. But somehow Liam made her feel safe, and as they moved forward together in this erotic exploration of submission, she was freer with each passing day.

Each morning she had awakened in Liam's arms, and he had made love to her before breakfast. After a light morning meal of bread and fruit, they swam and relaxed by the water, soaking in the sun and watching the waves dance to the shore. Liam permitted Shea to wear her bikini bottoms, and he wore swim trunks that hugged his sexy ass and muscular thighs. He would have her lie on a large, thick towel while he carefully applied sunscreen to every bare inch of her body. She would bask in his touch, unable to recall a time in her life when she'd been so still or felt so cherished. Despite the sunscreen, even after only three days her skin was bronze, her cheeks kissed with sun.

After a while Liam would turn to her and say, "It's time, Shea."

Her heart would immediately slip into overdrive, her nipples perking to attention, her sex moistening. He would take her back inside and lead her to the dungeon. There, he introduced her to the flogger, nipple clamps, extended bondage sessions, hot wax and more orgasms than she could count. She had learned ten basic slave positions, and could now handle the larger of the two anal plugs for long periods with relative ease, though she still remained squeamish and embarrassed when forced to endure examinations of her ass while bent over, legs spread, hands gripping her ankles for balance.

"We are working to desensitize you to this excessive modesty regarding your ass and this pretty little asshole" he would say as he probed her while she tried not to squirm. He had slipped a second lubricated finger inside her tight passage as he said this, and Shea had to admit it actually felt kind of good. "One day, when you're ready," he told her, "you will ask me to fuck your ass. Not because I require or demand it, but because you want it."

Shea had been at once relieved and curiously disappointed by this pronouncement. On some level, she had wanted Liam to just *take* it, to "force" her to submit to anal sex. That way, she didn't have to make the decision. He would make it for them. Though he continued to examine, probe and tease her, he hadn't brought up the subject of anal sex again, and neither had she.

This morning was the first time Liam had brought her outside for training. He must have known the boat was coming, the rat! She could hear the murmur of two masculine voices and her heart began a wild flutter. She clenched the rope above her wrists and shifted her feet on the sand. It sounded as if the voices were coming closer!

Oh my god, oh my god, Shea thought wildly, recalling Scott's grizzled tan face as she imagined him checking her out, his eyes sweeping insolently over her naked body. Did Liam, or whoever usually worked this particular island, always show off their naked slave girls for Scott or whoever else happened by? More to the point, how did she feel about being put on display like a slave girl on an auction block in some Arabian Nights fairy tale?

If Liam wants it, I want it, a small voice whispered inside her, but she could barely hear it over the beating of her own heart. She drew in a deep breath and let it slowly out. Closing her eyes, she practiced the calming techniques they had been working on over the past several days as an integral part of her training.

"Breathe deep," Liam would say, when Shea began to struggle or resist something he was doing. "Use your grace to rise above the fear. Flow with the pain, make it a part of yourself and then transcend it. Empty your mind, open yourself to the experience."

Shea lifted her face to the sun and forced her fingers to release their death grip on the ropes. She focused on emptying her mind of everything but

Liam's handsome face. *Use your grace to rise above the fear...* In and out, slowly she filled her lungs and released the fresh, salty air. *In...and out. In...and out.*

Something touched her face. Shea's eyes flew open and she gave a small, startled cry. Liam was standing in front of her, his hand caressing her cheek. "Hi, beautiful girl. Are you thirsty?" Shea saw he was holding a bottle of water in his other hand.

"Yes," she said, her mouth suddenly parched. She couldn't help straining to see behind him. Was Scott there, a leer on his face?

Liam followed her gaze, his smile widening into a grin. "He's gone, Shea. Didn't you hear the boat leaving?"

"Oh," Shea said, unable to keep the relief out of her voice. "No, I must have been drifting."

"I appreciate very much your willingness this morning with regard to having someone else see you like this," Liam replied as he opened the bottle of water and tilted it to her lips. "But I confess, I feel rather possessive of you, my darling. I don't want anyone else to see your beautiful, naked body. You're mine, all mine."

At least until Sunday. Then what? She pushed away the thought. *Stay in the moment*, she reminded herself firmly.

She drank deeply of the cool, refreshing water, and Liam let her drink her fill. Then he set the bottle on the towel near her feet and picked up the cane. Shea shuddered as she stared at the black-handled implement. What had she been thinking when she had agreed to the caning? She must have been temporarily insane.

Liam whipped the cane lightly in front of her, smiling wickedly as the whooshing sound cut through the air. Though it stung, Shea had fallen in love with the thuddy stroke of the flogger, with its many tresses of soft suede sharply kissing her skin until she'd been transported to a kind of altered consciousness she could only describe as sublime. The cane was another thing altogether. Her gut clenched as she anticipated the cut of that thin, whippy rod against her ass.

"I changed my mind. I don't think I'm ready for this," she blurted.

Liam said nothing. He placed a hand on the back of her head as he dipped his head and touched her lips with his. He kissed her, gently at first, and then more insistently. As always happened when he kissed her, Shea melted, all resistance sliding away in the heat of her lust.

He cupped her pussy, his fingers stroking her into instant, throbbing desire. "I don't think you are ready, sub girl," Liam whispered throatily as he pushed a finger into her wetness. "I *know* you are."

Shea moaned in response against his mouth as he kissed her again. He was touching her in just the right way and soon the familiar shudder of an orgasm rose through her body. Then Liam stepped back, his hand falling away from her throbbing sex. "Not yet, greedy girl." He was smiling, his eyes bright with lust and power. "That will be for after. First the pain, and then the pleasure, sweetest girl."

Shea felt herself falling completely under Liam's masterful spell, as she always did at times like these. "Are you ready, sub girl?" Liam asked, again holding up the cane.

"Yes, Sir," she breathed, her ass tingling, her cunt throbbing.

With a nod, Liam moved behind her. "Breathe," he said softly, his mouth near her ear. "Let go and let the pain transform you."

Shea took in a deep, shuddering breath and let it out slowly. In…and out. In…and out. A calmness settled over her, complemented by the rise of that new, peculiar courage she had been discovering over these past few days in Liam's dungeon. She now understood on a visceral level what he had meant by "the courage to submit", and she was empowered in a way she had never been at any other time in her life, even when closing a multi-million dollar deal.

The first strokes were light—what Liam called "warming the skin". The sensation was almost pleasurable, at first. The pleasure soon eased into a slight sting that moved rapidly over her ass and the backs of her thighs. She could hear the sound of the tap-tap-tap of the rattan against her flesh. She could do this. It wasn't so bad. No worse than a cropping — easier than a paddling.

Then came the whooshing sound, and a split second later an explosion of fire over her left ass cheek. Shea screamed, jerking wildly in her restraints. A second line of fire ripped across her right cheek. She began to dance on the warm sand.

"Shh," Liam murmured. "You're doing beautifully. Remember your grace. Stay in position." The whipping eased, returning to a tap-tap-tapping of stinging but endurable strokes. "That's it," Liam said encouragingly. "You're ready to move to the next level. Fifteen strokes, Shea. I know you can do it."

Another searing stroke landed, this time catching both cheeks in its long reach. "That's one," Liam said. The cane whipped at her thighs. Shea screamed again. "That's two," Liam said calmly. And again. "Three." Once more. "Four."

"No!" Shea wailed. She was dancing again, twisting in the ropes in her vain effort to get away. She wanted to be graceful and brave, but her body would not cooperate. Still the cane whistled and struck, again and again.

And then it happened.

At the ninth stroke, it was as if a cloak of peace dropped over her tortured spirit and stinging flesh. She actually felt it draping over her as her body stilled, her heart and gasping breath slowing and easing. Her head fell back of its own accord, her eyes closing, her lips parting softly, her face lifting toward the warm and welcoming sun.

The cane landed just as hard as before, its bite announced with a hiss a fraction of a second before it made contact. But this time Shea didn't scream. She didn't move. It hurt just as much, and yet the pain somehow transmuted upon impact into a deep, flowing heat that enveloped her in its sensual embrace.

She could hear the sound of the ocean as it lapped the shore nearby. She could hear her heart, its steady thump-thump just beneath the slow, even sound of her breathing. Dimly, as if he were far away, she could hear Liam counting the strokes.

His hand cupped her sex as his lips touched hers as lightly as rose petals. A deep tremor moved through her as he stroked her clit while pressing his fingers deep inside her. The heat on her skin moved inward, erupting into an orgasm that consumed her in its all-encompassing flames.

When she opened her eyes, she was half-sitting, half-lying on her back on the towel, cradled in Liam's arms. He was sitting up behind her. Her ass and thighs were stinging, but she found the sting pleasurable, and she wished suddenly they were inside so she could find a mirror and twist back to see the marks she knew must be there.

"You okay?" Liam said. "You left the world for a little while."

Left the world. That was it exactly. She had flown, soaring high over the ocean, free as a bird with the wind in her face. How to explain this? What words could she use that would make any sense? She opened her mouth to reply, but no sound issued. Instead, she twisted around so she could see Liam's face. She smiled at him, hoping somehow he would understand the incredible gift he'd given her. What more could he possibly do to top that incredible experience?

"I love you," he said softly, gazing down at her.

"Oh," she replied, grinning foolishly. That's what.

~*~

"I can't believe we've been here a week already," Shea said, echoing Liam's thoughts. It was Saturday night, and they were sharing their last dinner, enjoying it out on the veranda beneath a sky studded with stars against the backdrop of the water. "I can't believe I have to be at work on Monday morning. I think I could stay here forever."

"Our own private island in paradise," Liam agreed, thinking about the appointments he had scheduled for next week, and returning to the muggy heat of a Houston summer. He put down his wineglass and reached over to place his hand on Shea's. "It doesn't have to end, you know. We can create our own private paradise wherever we are. This is just the beginning."

Shea smiled, though her eyes were troubled. "You don't know what my life's like," she said. "I routinely work twelve to fifteen hour days sometimes, weekends included. I barely have time to breathe."

"Breathing's important," Liam said, trying to keep things light.

"Yeah." Shea gave a small laugh. "You sure have taught me that this week."

"Seriously," Liam continued, "I understand how busy you are. But isn't the whole reason you got shipped off on this vacation by your boss because you work too hard and too long? You're going to burn out if you keep up that pace." He pressed his lips together to keep from saying more. He had no right to demand that Shea alter her life or her business to accommodate him. That decision had to be hers.

"I know. I know you're right. Something has to change." She put her other hand over his. "Maybe you can help me learn to change it."

It was early, dawn just turning the sky outside a translucent indigo edging into lavender, but Liam was wide awake. He would be exhausted by the end of the day, but he didn't want to waste another moment sleeping, not on their last morning together on the island. Shea's back was to him, her dark, wavy hair cascading over the white pillow, her shoulder bare above the sheet.

The past week had been a marvel, and to say he didn't want it to end was the understatement of the century. As he lay pondering the unexpected development of falling in love with a client from Paradise Islands, something that had certainly never happened before, he tried to prepare for possible disappointment once Shea returned to her "real life."

He'd seen the phenomenon before—women caught in the heady throes of a D/s experience sometimes confused the tumult of emotions submission could bring with love. It was a kind of transference that had little to do with the actual Dom, and more to do with the experience he offered. Shea was so new to all of this. She was a natural student, and her eagerness to learn was breathtakingly exciting, but did it equate with love?

Shea rolled over, her eyes opening as she focused on Liam's face. "Hey, you," she said softly. "Can't sleep?"

He reached for her, pulling her into his arms. "Not really," he admitted.

She snuggled against his chest and they lay quietly for a while. "I know a cure for insomnia," she said with a giggle. She wriggled back a bit and reached for his cock, which quickly hardened as she stroked his shaft and balls. Lowering her head, she took him into her mouth, her warm, flickering tongue making him groan. He let her kiss and suckle him for a while, and then pushed her gently away, pressing her onto her back.

"No," she said suddenly.

Liam lifted his eyebrows, confused. Shea reached across him to his night table. She pulled open the drawer and pulled out the tube of lubricant and set it on the bed beside him. Throwing back the sheets, she shifted, maneuvering herself to her hands and knees.

"Like this," she said. Shea bit her lower lip in that cute way she had when she was nervous but determined, and Liam understood.

"Say it," he said, feeling himself slip fully into Dom mode. "Tell me precisely what it is you want."

"I want," she said, her voice wavering slightly, "for you to fuck my ass, Sir. Please." She drew in a breath, wincing slightly as if expecting to be hit.

Liam regarded Shea for a long moment. "Are you sure?"

She nodded, pressing her lips into a thin line, looking anything but sure. Then her chin lifted, and she wiggled her gorgeous ass in clear invitation. Not wanting to make her think he doubted her, Liam took the lubricant and smeared it over his shaft.

Shea had turned forward, so he couldn't see her face. Crouching behind her, he trailed his lubricated index finger down the cleft of her ass and circled it around the puckered hole. Shea stiffened, though she stayed in position. Liam pressed his finger carefully into the hot passage. He moved it slowly inside her until he felt her relax. He added a second finger, again taking his time until he felt the resistance draining away.

Finally he lifted himself behind her and pulled her ass against his groin. Gripping her hip with one hand, he guided the head of his cock between her cheeks. Before he even made contact, Shea squealed, jerking suddenly away from him.

Falling forward, she whipped her head back, her face twisted with anxiety. "I can't!" she cried breathlessly. "I'm sorry, I thought I was ready. I'm not. I can't. Don't make me!" She curled on her side, her back to him.

Liam lay down beside her and gathered her into his arms. "Shh, it's okay, Shea," he said, stroking her hair. "Of course I won't make you. You'll be ready when you're ready. It's okay, I promise."

She let out a deep, shuddering breath and he felt the tension uncoiling from her body as they lay together. His cock was still hard, pressed against her luscious ass. Unable to resist, he cupped her breasts, finding and fondling her nipples, which stiffened between his fingers.

Reaching between her legs, he found the still-hard nubbin of her clit and stroked it with a feather-soft touch. With a languorous sigh, Shea shifted against him until she was on her back, her legs falling open. Liam continued to stroke her sex until her face softened and grew slack with pleasure.

Liam's cock was now the consistency of steel. His hand still buried between her legs, Liam pushed Shea onto her side and maneuvered his cock between her legs from behind. One day, when she was ready, she would ask him to take her in the ass. Meanwhile, he was more than happy to sink his erection into the wet, hot clutch of her perfect cunt.

She groaned as he found his way into the small, wet opening and eased himself inside. He kept his hand at her sex as he began to thrust inside her. He moved slowly at first, until his need overcame consideration. Shea trembled against him, her cunt gripping him like a silken sheath while her small, breathy cries drove him mad with lust.

Through an act of sheer will, he held back his own orgasm, waiting for her. When she began to mewl and gasp, he couldn't even wait for her to ask for permission. "Come for me, sub girl. Now." Within seconds she began to shudder and buck against him, her movement spinning him over the cliff of a powerful orgasm.

They remained locked together, her back pressed against his chest, his cock still nestled inside her, as they both drifted in post-coital bliss, curled together like twin parentheses. Liam realized he must have dozed for a while, because he jolted suddenly awake, filled with a sense of disquiet, as if this whole week had only been a dream.

"If it is dream," he thought he heard Shea say, "then it's a damn good dream."

Startled, he lifted his head to see Shea's face, but she was fast asleep, a smile on her face.

Chapter 11

Shea returned to one hundred thirty-two unread emails and an inbox piled with reports, memos and files. It being six thirty on Monday morning, the office was still quiet, only Shea and Howard Williams, who always arrived at the crack of dawn, at their desks.

On their final morning, not wanting to leave him, even for a few hours, Shea had said, "Let's travel back to Texas together." Liam's eyes had crinkled in that delightful way they had in the seconds before a smile lit up his face. The smile had fallen away as he explained he had to stay for several more hours to close the bungalow and settle up paperwork with the behind-the-scenes catering and cleaning staff that made the paradise vacations possible. Shea had shocked herself by suggesting she change her return flight plans in order to remain with Liam. In the end, though, they hadn't been able to get it arranged on such short notice, and Shea had been spirited away in the boat, leaving a waving Liam behind as if he were part of the island, just part of a dream.

There had been delays at the airport due to a storm system moving through, and then the usual snarl of traffic once she finally made it back to Houston. Throughout the trip, the usually level-headed and calm Shea had careened from a bubbling happiness that threatened to unmoor her from the earth to a peculiar sense of foreboding, as if the limitless possibilities that had been opened up during her amazing week in paradise would be lost once real life came banging again on her door.

The foreboding had lifted the moment she heard Liam's clipped British accent on the phone that night. "I can't wait to see you again," he had said with a puppy dog eagerness that made her smile. Suddenly work, for all its satisfaction and challenge, was no longer her reason, or at least not her only reason, for living. For the first time in her life, she wished Monday would never come, and yet it had, and all too soon.

With a resolute sigh, she clicked open her email and began to sort through the messages as she sipped at her coffee. She had nearly finished going through her inbox when a cheese Danish suddenly appeared on the edge of her desk. She looked up to find Jackie standing over her. "Look at you, all tan and rested. Aunt Jackie always knows best. Did you have a good time?"

Shea couldn't stop her broad smile. "I did. It was the most amazing experience of my life."

Jackie lifted her finely arched eyebrows and then waggled them like Grouch Marx while holding an air cigar between thumb and forefinger to her lips. "I want to hear every detail, and then I have something very exciting to share with you." She began to walk away, turning back to add, "My office in twenty."

When Shea tapped at Jackie's open door, Jackie, on the phone, nodded and waved Shea into the room. Sitting in the aggressively air-conditioned corner suite, Shea stared out the window at the downtown skyline and the broad flat plains of the Texas horizon beyond, but what she saw instead was the endless blue of the Caribbean Sea. She imagined Liam beside her on the sand, the sun gleaming against his tan, muscular body, his deep brown eyes gazing into hers as he dipped his head to kiss her…

"Earth to Shea, earth to Shea." Jackie's strident voice broke through Shea's reverie and she jerked toward the sound.

"I'm sorry, what? I—I must have been daydreaming."

"No kidding." Jackie smirked. "So, do I have your full attention now?" She glanced at her watch. "I have exactly twenty-two minutes until the meeting with Shepherd Software Solutions. You have five minutes to fill me in on your hedonistic adventures and then I want to throw something out there for your consideration."

Shea frowned. "My consideration? What? What are you talking about?"

Jackie waved a finger in Shea's direction as she shook her head. "Nope. You first. I sprang for the vacay so I want to hear the juicy details. Was the boy toy they chose for you everything the brochure promised? Did he wine and dine you, give you massages and pedicures, and even better, tuck you in at night?"

"Oh, well. I, uh…" Where to begin? Did she tell Jackie what had really transpired? Would Jackie freak out? Maybe she'd just tell her a sort of glossed-over version. After all, she couldn't expect Jackie to understand what she herself hadn't understood until Liam Jordan had introduced her to a world of possibility she'd never even dreamed of.

"Whoa, it must have better than I thought," Jackie said, laughing. "I've never seen you at a loss for words, Shea. Come on, you can tell me."

"Well," Shea said, deciding to plunge in. "There were kind of some crossed wires at first. They thought I had signed up for the BDSM abduction package."

"They what? Oh my god, what a nightmare!" Jackie interjected, bringing her hands to her face.

"Well, yeah, kind of. Except not really. I mean…" What had she been thinking? How could she possibly explain within the allotted timeframe that Liam had become not only her lover, but her Dom? How could she make Jackie understand the power and passion of an erotic exchange of power? Should she even try?

Dialing back, she said, "It worked out okay, really. Liam figured out the mistake and we had a great week. The island was incredible, Jackie—all that clear, blue water and white sand. The bungalow we stayed in was really nice and the food—"

"Forget all that." Jackie leaned forward. "Tell me about this Liam guy. Was he a total hunk? Did he, uh, service you properly? Is this Paradise Islands gig for the woman with everything but time really all it's cracked up to be? Should I be booking a week for myself, Jerry be damned?"

"It was pretty fantastic," Shea admitted. "You know I was skeptical, but I have to say, that was the best gift anyone ever gave me, Jackie. It's really changed my life." Shea sighed happily. "Liam is so…amazing. I've never met anyone like him. He's British and he has this sexy accent. He's tall and built and maybe the sexiest guy I ever met. He's the most…I mean, I never knew I…um. That is…"

"Oh. My. Fucking. God." Jackie leaned forward across her desk, her mouth hanging open. "No. No, no, no. No way. Girlfriend, don't tell me. You didn't actually *fall* for this guy, did you?"

Shea started to retort that she had not only fallen for him, she was head over heels in love. But as she took in Jackie's incredulous expression, the words died in her throat.

"Shea, sweetie." Jackie's tone became solicitous, the concern evident on her face. "Look. I know it's been a long time since you were involved with a guy. So maybe it's just the novelty of it. Or the fact that this guy paid lots of yummy attention to you for a solid week against the backdrop of a luxury tropical island. Hey"—she lifted her hands palms up—"I get it. Look, I'm really glad you had a good time, but honey, this guy was *paid* to give you a good time. This week he'll be paid to give someone else a good time. Surely you're aware of that?"

Shea could feel her cheeks growing hot. A sharp jab of unease pricked the edges of her happiness. Could Jackie be right? Now that the week was over, was whatever they'd shared over too? As quickly as the unwelcome thought entered her brain, she shook it away. Jackie just didn't understand. How could she possibly, when Shea herself was still working to wrap her head around the amazing events of the past week?

"Not to worry," Jackie continued, blithely unaware of Shea's internal conversation. "Now that we've established you're not made of stone, I have a guy in mind I really want you to meet."

Even if Liam weren't in the picture, Shea knew she had to cut this one off at the pass. "Jackie, you know how I feel about blind dates. Your intentions are good but—"

Jackie held up a hand. "Just hear me out. His name is Peter Roden and he's really cute. He's American but he spends most of the year in London, so he'd be perfect for you. I'll explain why in just a second." Again Shea made to interrupt, but Jackie barreled on. "He's recently divorced but they were separated for ages so it's not like you'd be a rebound girlfriend. He's forty-two." Again Shea opened her mouth and again Jackie raised her hand. "I know, I know, it's a little old, but he's a young forty-two. Works out, all that stuff. He's in import and export—a family business. He's easily worth—"

"Jackie, stop," Shea finally managed to interject. "I'm not in the market for a guy. Especially not someone who lives overseas most of the year. Liam and I—"

"Shea, sweetie," Jackie interrupted. "No offense, but you need to get off that. This Liam guy is a fantasy. He doesn't exist in real life." She offered a sympathetic smile, and then pulled herself upright in a way Shea recognized as her "time to get on with business" mode, as she continued, "I have something way more important to discuss with you than men. It's the opportunity of a lifetime."

At that moment, Shea's cell phone, which she'd slipped into her suit jacket before coming to Jackie's office, buzzed. Taking it from her pocket, she saw the text from Liam: *Beautiful girl. I can't stop thinking about* you. *Counting the hours until tonight.* She nearly held out the phone as proof that Liam most certainly did exist, but for the moment she held her tongue, her curiosity now piqued by Jackie's pronouncement.

Jackie lifted her brows. "Both Richard Fielding and John Harris were in the running for this promotion, but Howard, Dave and I all agreed you were best suited for the position."

That got Shea's full attention. "Promotion? I didn't realize we had any vacancies in upper management. What are you talking about?"

Jackie leaned back in her chair and smiled. "You know we've been talking about expanding into Europe and Asia for a while now. It's finally come through. Top brass is ready to make the move. You have been tapped to help open our new office in London."

"Oh," Shea breathed, momentarily stunned by this unexpected announcement.

"The only negative"—Jackie leaned forward and lowered her voice—"is that Howard Williams is going too. You'll be reporting directly to Mr. Personality himself." She grinned. "As you know, he spent time in London before joining Sutton Investments, and he still has some connections there. We'll talk more about the details, of course," Jackie continued, "but if you accept the position, the two of you will fly out next Monday. I know it's kind of sudden, but apparently the timing is right and we need to strike while the iron is hot."

Shea stared speechlessly at Jackie, her world suddenly titled on its axis by this unexpected opportunity being dumped into her lap at the worst possible time.

Jackie tilted her head appraisingly at Shea. "I thought you'd be dancing on the desk at the news. Isn't this what you've always wanted?" When Shea didn't immediately respond, Jackie added, "I know it's a lot to absorb, and yeah, Howard is a slave driver, but you give him a run for his money in terms of clocking in the hours, so that shouldn't be an issue for you. The position comes with a sizable salary increase, plus significant bonus opportunities." Jackie slapped the desk. "This is it, Shea! The dream job you've been waiting for. I'll miss you like crazy, but I couldn't possibly stand in the way of such an incredible opportunity." She beamed expectantly.

Jackie was right. This was the opportunity of a lifetime. She'd always wanted to travel and had even seriously considered taking a job with a rival firm in London not two years before, but Jackie had convinced her to stay on with Sutton Investments.

If she hadn't just spent the most amazing week of her life with Liam, she would have been over the moon with excitement. But how could she leave Liam and the promise of continuing her submissive exploration? She thought of Liam's smile, of his touch, of the deep and powerful connection she'd felt when submitting to his sensual commands. Though her rational brain whispered that it was too soon, for the first time in her life she had found someone she could imagine growing old with. How could she choose between her career, which up until last week had been the most important thing in her life, and Liam Jordan?

Not willing to share all the galloping thoughts charging through her head, she voiced the least important of them. "What about my Houston client base? I have several deals still in the works."

"Oh, don't worry about that." Jackie waved her hand airily. "You know the guys will swoop like vultures on whatever you've got going. You've worked your ass off for this firm. It's time it paid you back." She looked down at the diamond encrusted wedding ring on her left hand and then back up at Shea. "You're the perfect person for the job, what with no husband or kids or anything to get in your way. Take a day or two and mull it over if you need to. Dave and Howard want to meet with you on Wednesday morning. You can give us your decision then."

Jackie stood and walked around her desk. She held out her arms, and Shea stood, allowing herself to be enveloped in Jackie's signature *Joy* perfume as

Jackie pulled her close. "Congrats, sweetie. I'm so proud of you."

~*~

Anne knelt on the yoga mat in Liam's training room in classic waiting pose, her knees spread, hands resting palm up on her thighs. She wore a black leather bustier, her shaved pussy bare beneath it. She was staring demurely at the floor, though Liam knew she was listening to every word Barry and Liam were saying. Anne was small and blond, nothing like the tall, willowy and dark-haired Shea, yet Liam kept imagining her there in Anne's place.

It had been less than twenty-four hours, but Liam missed Shea as if they'd been apart for months. He was behaving like a teenager, texting her constantly throughout the day, and breaking into huge smiles each time she replied. He counted the hours until they would see each other again, and it was all he could do to give his clients the focus they deserved.

Finally Liam had made it to his last appointment of the day. He tried not to let his dislike for Barry come through during the session. From what Anne had said on the phone, Barry was one of those unfortunate men who believed all subs owed him their respect, admiration and instant obedience, simply by virtue of his being dominant. Though she claimed to love him, Anne had said Barry didn't pay attention to her cues, repeatedly pushing her too far and too fast. When she protested or asked for something different, Barry would inform her that he was the Master and she was the slave, and he would decide what she needed and what she could handle.

Yet Liam had to give credit where it was due. After all, Barry had agreed to come for training, albeit reluctantly. Apparently Anne had issued an ultimatum—get some training, or find a new sub. During the interview that had taken up the first fifteen minutes of their session, Barry had agreed to whatever Liam decided was appropriate for the rest of the hour-long session, but Liam was pretty sure he wasn't going to like what came next.

Barry was holding a long, thin rattan cane that he kept whipping through the air, grinning evilly each time Anne winced at the sound. "When she's not being a resistant little brat, my slave can take sixty licks. Sometimes we draw blood. It's so fucking hot to know I did that to her. I tie her down so she doesn't get out of position. She whines and moans the whole time, but she loves it. She loves that I love it and she always gets a great orgasm afterward, right, slave?"

"Yes, Sir," the girl replied from her position on the yoga mat, though her endorsement lacked much enthusiasm.

"She loves that you love it," Liam echoed. "That's not quite the same thing as loving the cane. Most subs I know who claim to love the cane, love it all the time except when they're actually being caned. Because it hurts like hell. They like where it can take them, but the actual cut of the cane can be extremely painful. Am I right, Anne?"

"Yes, Sir!" Anne replied, this time with such force that Liam had to smile.

Turning back to Barry, he continued, "It's especially important when administering corporal punishment that you really pay attention to your sub's body. You need to carefully control your delivery, and you need to back off when there are signs of real distress."

Liam walked over to Anne and moved in a slow circle around her. Reaching down, he traced the line of a scar on her back, one of many that marred her pale skin. "Is this scar from the cane?"

Anne started to reply, but Barry overrode her. "It's a badge of courage. That's what we call it. Anne is proud to carry the permanent marks of her submission. They're a sign of respect for her Master."

Liam pressed his lips together to keep from saying what he really thought. He tried never to judge what two people who were part of a consensual relationship did to each other, as long as it was truly consensual. But clearly Anne, who had managed to drag Barry to this training session, wasn't entirely happy with the arrangement.

Liam turned to Barry. "Have you ever been caned, Barry?"

Barry looked confused. "What? Me? Of course not. I'm the Master. I dole out the punishment. She takes it."

"I understand," Liam replied calmly. "But it's important when you are responsible for someone's training and wellbeing that you know precisely what it is you are asking them to endure. I'm going to give you ten strokes so you can gain a better understanding of what it is Anne is willing to suffer for you."

"What the fuck?" Barry sputtered.

Liam lifted his eyebrows. "You routinely give Anne sixty, didn't you just say that?" Liam took the cane from Barry's hand and walked to the spanking bench. "Surely a big, strong man like you can handle ten strokes?"

Barry's face was brick red. He glowered at his slave girl. "Did you put him up to this?"

"No, she didn't," Liam interjected. "Though not everyone agrees with my philosophy, I feel strongly that a good Dom never asks anything of his sub that he can't handle himself."

"Nobody's going to cane me. I'm a Dom, not some pussy sub boy."

"There's no shame in what I'm asking you to do, Barry. As you noted yourself, it takes courage to submit." Speaking in a gentler tone, he added, "Anne's not happy, Barry. That's why you're here. I want to help you learn how to make her happy. She loves you. Don't you want to be worthy of that love?"

Barry's face crumpled and he nodded. He walked hesitantly to the bench and, with a last look at Anne, unbuckled his belt and pulled down his pants.

"Underwear, too," Liam said.

To his credit, Barry obeyed without further protest. Liam moved behind him and placed a hand lightly on his lower back. "Now, just relax and flow with the pain."

Liam brought the cane down with moderate force, hard enough to leave a mark. Barry howled, immediately bringing his hands back to cover his ass. Liam glanced toward Anne, who, though her eyes were demurely focused on the ground, couldn't quite hide her smile.

By the time Liam finished administering the last stroke, Barry was gritting his teeth and blinking back tears. "Jesus," he swore. "That fucking hurts. I didn't realize how much."

Liam stepped back, waiting while Barry pulled his pants back up. "It does. And since you're probably not a sensual masochist, there was no pleasure associated with the pain. But you should understand, even though Anne processes the pain differently than you do, it still hurts her just as much."

Barry nodded soberly. Liam continued, "That's why it's important you understand just exactly what it is you ask of her. It's appropriate in a consensual Master/slave relationship for you to ask all she can give, but not more than she can give. Do you see the difference?"

"Yeah," Barry muttered. He walked over to Anne and reached down, lifting her into his arms. "I'm gonna do better, baby, I promise," Liam heard him say as she buried her face against his chest. Turning back to Liam, he said, "Uh, can we schedule another couple of sessions? You know, just to make sure I get it right."

As if she'd timed it, Liam's cell phone buzzed with a phone call just as Liam was saying his goodbyes to the couple and closing the door. Trying to keep his feet from lifting off the ground in his excitement, he slid his finger over the screen to accept the call. "Hey there, Shea. Perfect timing. I've just finished up for the day. I can't wait to see you. Are you back at your place? Still at the office? Want me to come pick you up?"

Shea's laugh was warm. "There's nothing I would like better. I think I can get out of here by seven. Could you be at my place by about 7:30? Does that work for you?"

"Like a charm. There's a new Italian place in Montrose I've been wanting to try. Or we could go to a new sushi place over on Kirby Drive that's been getting rave reviews."

"Either one sounds great," Shea replied. "Surprise me. But Liam," her voice dropped suddenly, "there's something I have to discuss with you. Something about work."

"Is everything okay?"

"Oh, yeah. Sure, yes. Fine. It's just—I got an offer." She gave a nervous laugh. "One of those kinds it's very hard to refuse. I wanted to talk it over with you."

"Sounds intriguing. Tell me."

Shea paused and then said, "I—I'd rather wait until we're face to face."

Then why bring it up? Was she going to drop some bomb on him? Now that she was back on her home turf, was she reconsidering the wisdom of continuing where they'd left off? How long had it been since he cared so much? Everything was still so sparklingly new between them, and yet he felt more sure about Shea and the instant place she'd found in his heart than he ever had about anything in his life.

He had insisted on her trust as they'd explored her submissive impulses together over the past amazing week. Surely he could afford her the same trust? She had something she needed to talk about, and she wanted to do it face to face. It wouldn't do to pressure her to speak before she was ready. His job at that moment was to be there for her, plain and simple, with no strings attached.

"I shall count the minutes until 7:30," Liam replied, forcing a lightness into his tone. "Then you can tell me all about this offer of yours."

"Thank you, Liam," Shea replied, something in her tone shooting another arrow of unease straight into Liam's gut. "See you soon."

Chapter 12

Shea watched the silver BMW pull up in front of her condo, her heart catching when she saw it was Liam. She had wanted to shower and take her time getting ready before he arrived, but work, as usual, had taken over, gobbling up the time like some ravenous monster. When she'd finally managed to pull things together enough to leave, she'd barely had time to crawl through traffic, fling her briefcase down and pull on something less austere than her usual tailored work suit.

While waiting at the office elevators, she had been met by none other than Dave Sutton himself. In his usual larger-than-life fashion, he'd smacked her on the back, loudly congratulating her on her upcoming assignment. Startled by his pronouncement since she hadn't even formally accepted the position, Shea had murmured something noncommittal to Dave's already retreating back.

She was being offered her dream job—with a chance to travel overseas, and more money than she knew what to do with. It should have been a no-brainer. There would have been no question, no hesitation, if it hadn't been for the tall, sexy guy now striding toward her front door. Before Liam had burst into her life, she would never have believed that anyone or anything could derail her from following the thrilling trajectory of her career.

Until Jackie had forced her to take that vacation in paradise, Shea hadn't known there could be anything more satisfying than closing a well-constructed deal. Though she hadn't been conscious of doing it, she had put her emotions in a kind of deep freeze, focusing her passions instead on being the best and brightest in her chosen career, with no sacrifice too great in the name of advancement. She had thought the kind of excitement and, yes, the love she'd experienced in the short but amazing week with Liam existed only on the pages of romance novels.

She'd spent the afternoon in a confused daze, ping-ponging between stunned excitement at the opportunity that was being dangled before her, and a sinking heart at the thought of leaving Liam behind if she accepted the assignment. She kept trying to tell herself that a week in paradise did not equal real life, but in her heart she knew it had been the most real thing she'd ever experienced.

Liam was the first man who had ever managed to reach past the thicket of brambles that had grown up around her heart over the years. He was the first person around whom she had felt safe to cry since she was a little girl. The first man who had helped her tap into something in the core of her nature that she doubted she would ever have had the courage or understanding to explore on her own. Beyond all that, he was the first man she could love, really love, with every part of her being.

How could she just walk away from that, from him?

She watched Liam head up the path toward the front door, her heart fluttering with anticipation. It was strange to see him dressed in something other than shorts or swim trunks, but she liked what she saw very much. He was wearing black jeans and a white shirt opened at the throat that contrasted nicely with his tan skin. She loved the way he moved, his stride powerful and confident. He saw her in the window and his face split into a wide smile, his eyes crinkling into half moons as he lifted a hand in a wave.

Shea sprinted to the front door and yanked it open. "Shea," Liam said, the word like a caress. He held out his arms and Shea stepped into them, reveling in his warm, enveloping embrace. Though they'd been apart for less than forty-eight hours, tears of relief and happiness pricked her eyelids. Liam dipped his head to kiss her lips, and for the first time since they'd parted, all thoughts slipped out of Shea's head, her entire being consumed with his kiss.

When he finally let her go, Shea had to resist the impulse to reach for him and pull him back down. Forget dinner—she wanted to yank him inside, pull off his clothes and make love then and there. He held something up and she saw it was a bouquet of flowers wrapped in green tissue paper. "For you," he said, grinning.

"They're beautiful. Thank you." Shea beamed back at him. "Come in and I'll just put them in water before we go."

Liam followed her into the house and on into the kitchen. He leaned against a counter, watching her as she retrieved a vase and filled it with water. "So, how was your first day back on the job? Did they run you ragged?"

"No more than usual." Shea smiled at him as she finished arranging the pretty purple, yellow and orange flowers. "Though I paid the price, of course, for being away for a week. I was hoping the work fairies would have handled the piles of crap in my inbox and my email, but I must have got the magic spell wrong, because it was all there when I got back."

Liam laughed and moved closer, taking Shea once more into his arms. She was wearing a pale yellow silk tank top and matching jacket over a black skirt, and as Liam held her, his hands slid beneath her top, his touch electrifying her. He pulled her close, so her breasts were pressed against his chest. "I missed you," he said, nuzzling her ear. His hands moved down, sliding over her ass. He moved with her until she was leaning against the kitchen table. Wrapping his arms around her, he lifted her onto the table and stepped between her legs, forcing them apart with his body. He leaned in again, crushing her mouth with his. She could feel his erection against her damp panties and she moaned.

As he kissed her his hand slid between them, his fingers tugging her silky panties aside and slipping into her wetness. He continued to kiss her as he pulled open his jeans.

"Liam," Shea gasped against his insistent mouth, "what are you doing?" But she knew what he was doing, and what's more, she wanted it. Desperately.

He answered, "I'm claiming you, Shea. I must have you. You belong to me."

"Yes," she hissed, drawing out the word as the head of his cock nudged itself between her swelling labia. He pushed inside her, his hard, thick cock nearly hurting her, but she didn't care. She needed him too much to care. She wrapped her legs around his hips to pull him in deeper. He slammed inside her, the impact pushing her backward on the table. But his strong arms caught her, holding her close.

He was breathing hard. His pubic bone was angled perfectly so it stroked her clit with each delicious thrust of his cock. Though it seemed impossible, within seconds Shea was ready to climax. Her body began to tremble and she held tight to Liam as he thrust and swiveled inside her.

"Oh god," she groaned, "I'm going to come."

"Ask," he hissed in her ear, and she remembered then. On the island he had always had her ask permission before she orgasmed. All the memories came flooding back in that moment — the wild sex, the intense erotic torture sessions, the deeply sensual caning on the beach, with the warm sun, the salty breeze and her Master taking her to a place she never knew existed.

"Please," she begged breathlessly. "Let me come, Sir."

"Yes," he grunted. She could feel the heat emanating from his body, as if a flame had been lit inside him. His dark eyes burned with a fierce passion that was almost frightening. "Yes. Come, baby. Now." He shuddered and slammed into her, the force of impact hurling her over the edge of a long, powerful orgasm. She remained anchored to the earth only by his strong, sure embrace as he cradled her in his arms.

Liam lifted Shea from the table, his cock still buried inside her. He carried her into the living room and settled on the sofa, positioning Shea so she was facing him on his lap. She rested her head on his shoulder as a delicious, deep peace settled over her. They rested that way a while until their hearts slowed, their breathing returning to normal.

Shea shifted a little on Liam's lap and his cock slid out of her. She flopped over to the sofa beside him, pushing back the hair from her damp forehead.

"Whew," she said with a small laugh. "That was some hello. I'm going to need to change my panties before we go to dinner."

Liam grinned. "I'm sorry. I don't know what came over me. Or rather"—his eyes crinkled—"I do know. You're so beautiful, Shea. I know that was a rather ungentlemanly display," he said in his cute British way, "but I couldn't wait another minute to have you. I think I would have actually died. Keeled over right on the spot if I didn't sink my cock into your perfection."

Shea laughed, both embarrassed and pleased by this absurd declaration. "Well," she quipped, "we couldn't have you dying, could we? Then who would take me to dinner?"

"Oh," Liam said as he reached to zip his jeans and tuck in his shirt, "where are my manners? You must be starving." He stood and held out a hand. Shea took it, letting him pull her to her feet. "Let's go to dinner. I'm thinking the sushi place?"

Shea nodded enthusiastically. "Sounds perfect."

Liam reached for her shoulders. He stared down into her face with those liquid brown eyes. His voice deepened and though he spoke softly, she felt the authority, and her own softening response. "You will keep on those damp panties while we dine, as a reminder of who you belong to."

Shea opened her mouth to retort that no way in hell was she going to wear wet panties to dinner, but instead, she bit her lip as a submissive thrill coiled through her body, its impact as powerful as a double shot of hundred proof bourbon. She drew in a tremulous breath. "Yes, Sir," she whispered throatily and then, unaccountably, "Thank you, Sir."

~*~

As they made their way along the freeway toward the restaurant, Liam cast sidelong glances at the lovely woman beside him. He hadn't meant to make love to her before dinner, but his body had had other plans. Christ, he could not get enough of her. He never wanted to let her out of his sight, not even for a second, not ever.

They listened to a jazz station on the radio. As Liam drove, Shea fixed her hair and makeup in the vanity mirror, erasing the disheveled, just-been-fucked look he loved so well. When they exited the ramp at Westheimer and eased into the long line at the traffic light, he turned to look at her. Shea was staring out the front window, her lips pressed into a thin line, her hands twisting nervously in her lap.

Concerned, Liam said, "Hey, what is it? Are you okay?"

She glanced quickly at him and then looked away. "I'm nervous," she blurted.

"What for? What's the matter?"

She blew out a breath. "Remember, I said I had something to tell you. The offer I got today."

"Ah, yes," Liam replied. He had actually forgotten during the excitement of their lovemaking, but now the recollection returned in full force, along with the unease he had felt earlier. "So, tell me about this offer that's too good to refuse." He realized he was clenching the steering wheel and he forced his fingers to relax. He turned to smile at her. She was regarding him with those luminous blue-gray eyes that so transfixed him. He nodded his encouragement for her to continue.

After a moment, Shea said, "Until this week, this would have sent me to the moon. It's what I always wanted." She frowned. "Or what I thought I wanted." She bit her lower lip.

"Go on," Liam urged.

She lifted her chin, as if girding herself for what she had to say next. "I've been offered a promotion," she finally said. "A chance to help open a new office for the firm. I don't know all the details yet, but it means a lot more responsibility, and money too, of course. It's a huge vote of confidence by management."

"Wow, congratulations," Liam replied sincerely, his anxiety lifting. "Looks and brains too," he teased, though he meant it. "Seriously, though, what's the problem? That sounds fantastic."

The light turned and he eased forward a few car lengths before the light changed again to red. Shea looked at him miserably. "It's in London," she said heavily. "And they want me to fly out this coming Monday. It would mean moving. Leaving Houston. Leaving...you."

Liam felt as if someone had shot him in the gut, the shock of her revelation leaving him mute for several long seconds. The line of traffic snaked forward and this time he was finally able to turn left onto Westheimer, heading toward Kirby. His first instinct was to shout, "No! You can't go! You're mine!" But how could he possibly say that?

Yes, they were definitely on the path to something amazing, but Shea was being offered what he recognized as the chance of a lifetime, and no doubt something she really wanted. How could he stand in the way of that? Even for a second?

"It sounds like an incredible opportunity," he finally said. "Something you would be crazy to turn down. I mean, if that's what you want, of course." He glanced at her and then back at the traffic. She was staring straight ahead now, her hands still twisting in her lap. He reached over and placed his hand over hers, squeezing gently. "Shea, darling, I think this is something you should explore. London is a great place to live, providing someone else is footing the bill." He forced a laugh. "I know how important your career is. You owe it to yourself to give this a chance."

"But what about us?" she blurted, grabbing hold of his hand and gripping it in both hers. "What about our D/s exploration? How can I just leave all that? How could I leave *you* just like that?"

Liam smiled, pushing down his selfish desire to forbid her to leave him, even for a second. "Sweetest girl, you won't be leaving me. That's one of the perks of having my own business—I have some flexibility. Once you're settled and ready, just say the word and I'll fly over to see you. I can introduce you to some friends I have in London. We can check out the scene there. It'll be great."

"But then what? Eventually you'll have to return to Texas."

"For a while, I suppose. I imagine you would be pretty busy getting the office up and running, and figuring out if this is something you really want to do." He pulled the car into the restaurant's large parking lot, pleased to see an open spot not too far from the door. He slid into it, cut the engine and turned to face Shea. "Have you already accepted the position?"

Shea shook her head. "No. They're giving me a couple of days to mull it over. Jackie gave me a prospectus to read with all the details, and I'm to meet with top management on Wednesday."

"That's a good thing, then. You have a few days to let it sink in."

"Yeah, but there's still the issue of *us*, Liam. You and me."

Liam reached for Shea's hands, taking them in his. He felt the warm, strong feeling in his heart that he understood was love, a love that was new for him in that it was ready to give of itself without expectation of anything in return. Pushing away the more selfish impulse that existed alongside the love, that of insisting she drop everything in her life and devote herself exclusively to him, 24/7, Liam said, "Want to know what I think?"

Shea nodded, fixing her wide, beautiful eyes on his face.

"From what I know of you and how hard you've worked in your career, this is a chance of a lifetime, something you owe it to yourself to try. Having let a few opportunities pass in my life that I later came to regret, I would hate to see that happen to you." *Even though I want to get on my knees right now and beg you not to go.* Mentally Liam shook his head and ordered himself to cut it out. Not everything was about what *he* wanted. And it was a recipe for disaster to insist she stay, if she did so just for him.

Liam made himself smile as he continued, "Taking this assignment doesn't mean you are committing to move to the UK for the rest of your life, or that your moving means the end of you and me. It just means you're giving yourself a chance to try something you've earned. It's a chance to move up to the ranks of management, and prove to yourself you've got what it takes to become a major player in your field. Am I right?"

"Well, yeah," Shea admitted. "I mean, it's an incredible opportunity, but—"

"No buts, then. You won't lose me, not if you don't want to. Don't forget, I'm from England myself. If this seems like something you want to stick with for a while, and it still makes sense for us, I can definitely see myself moving back there, if it means being with you, Shea. I'm sure I can start my business again over there."

"You'd do that for me?"

Liam leaned over to kiss her soft lips. "I'd do anything for you, Shea. Anything at all."

Chapter 13

Shea had a cardinal rule never to sleep over at a guy's house for more than one night in a row. But what the hell, she told herself that Saturday morning with a grin—rules were made to be broken. The only time that week she'd been back to her place was to grab more clothing. Since their dinner Monday night, Liam and Shea had been inseparable. Excepting, of course, when she had to be at work.

Had to be at work! That was definitely a departure, and a rather disconcerting one, for Shea. Before Liam had come into her life, there was work, and there was preparing for work. When she did eventually leave the office, it was to run errands, do her exercise regime, review her schedule and projects for the following day, and grab what rest she could before the alarm went off the next morning.

Now, however, she would catch herself daydreaming in the middle of a complex analysis, or surreptitiously checking her watch when a meeting was going on longer than scheduled, cutting into her precious time with Liam. She had accepted the position to help start up the London office, despite conflicting feelings about leaving Liam so early in their relationship, but was she up to the task? Sometimes she worried she was losing her edge. How did other people manage to juggle their career and a relationship?

They don't work eighty hours a week, that's how.

This thought was a shocking one, and one Shea would have brushed off as unworthy once upon a time. But since being with Liam, she had begun to realize her one-track and all-consuming dedication to her career had come at a cost. Not only had she had no significant other in her life for some years now, she didn't really have any friends anymore, save for Jackie, who understood the pressure that came along with the job. Even Jackie had been warning her for some time now that all work and no play wasn't a good thing. But if Shea hadn't dedicated herself to such a degree, would she, one of the youngest people in the firm, and a female to boot, have been tapped for such a prestigious opportunity?

The awareness of her upcoming departure for England, while Liam remained behind at least for the foreseeable future, made each moment they shared that much more precious. Rather than rushing through her life to get to the next assignment or event, for the first time in memory, save of course for the week in paradise, Shea treasured every moment out of the office. She cherished her time with her man.

Her man! Liam was her man, no question about it. In the week since they'd been back in Texas, he had shown her with every word and action that he wanted her fully in his life. And while she loved the sweetness and closeness, she also craved the continuing exploration into erotic submission.

As Liam worked with her on position training, endurance, bondage and erotic pain, he had talked about full accessibility. "It's essential," he had said one evening while inspecting her body, "that a sub be fully accessible to her Dom at all times. You must hold nothing back, either physically or emotionally. To do so is to resist, and to resist is to disobey. Obedience, for a submissive, is the path to the truest form of release and happiness."

That was why now, as she stood beneath the spray of the hot shower, Shea took the bottle of baby oil she used to shave her legs and squirted a quantity onto her palm. She rubbed it onto her trimmed pubic hair and picked up the fresh razor. Slowly, carefully, she began to scrape away the hair on her mound and labia, rinsing the razor and adding more oil as she went, until she was smooth as silk.

Done with her shower, she climbed out of the tub and regarded herself in the full length mirror. She spread her legs into an at ease position, feet shoulder-width apart, arms at her sides, and stared at her fully denuded form, not sure if she liked the new bare look or not. Would Liam like it?

He chose that moment to enter the bathroom, and Shea quickly brought the towel around her body, not yet ready to show him what she'd done. He came up behind her and put his arms around her. "I made blueberry pancakes," he said, smiling at her in the mirror. "Hungry?"

Shea twisted back to face him. "You're going to make me fat," she laughed, tucking the towel into place.

"Not to worry," he replied. "I'll whip you into shape."

"Literally, I hope," she quipped.

"Absolutely." He reached for her towel, plucking it away from her body. Shea's heart clutched and she started to cover herself, but then let her arms fall to her sides. Liam took a step back as his gaze swept over her naked form. Shea felt her cheeks flush, but at the same time a small white-hot flame of passion kindled inside her as it always did when she experienced Liam's dominance, which emanated from him with a heat all its own.

Though her heart beat hard and fast, at the same time a submissive calm moved through her as she stood before her Dom. Locking her eyes on his, Shea lifted her arms and laced her fingers behind her head, assuming an at attention stance, breasts thrust proudly forward.

"Shea," Liam whispered, stepping closer. "You're so beautiful." He cupped her bare pussy in his large hand and it was all she could do to remain still, when what she really wanted to do was grind herself wantonly against his palm.

"It's an offering," she said, her voice coming out husky. She cleared her throat. "I—I wanted to be fully accessible to you, Sir."

Liam nodded, his eyes smoldering. "I understand. It's a beautiful gift. And perfect for what I have planned for you after breakfast. You're going to experience your first cunt whipping."

With the prospect of the upcoming session in the dungeon, Shea didn't have much appetite for breakfast, though she did manage to eat one blueberry pancake. Liam, on the other hand, put away three pancakes and four pieces of bacon. It was no surprise that she couldn't concentrate on her food, given that Liam had instructed her to remain naked during the meal so he could admire her completely nude body while he ate. "Spread your legs so I can see your gorgeous cunt," he said casually as he sipped at his second cup of coffee.

The irony was, while a small part of her brain wanted to bristle and refuse, Liam's command sent ripples of desire juddering through her frame, and she embarrassed herself by leaving a wet spot of lust on the wooden chair.

After breakfast, Liam took her by the hand and led her to the dungeon. His dungeon had more equipment than the one on the island, including a large web of black rubber strips with Velcro cuffs attached at several strategic locations, two cages—one tall and narrow, the other low to the ground with barely enough room to curl inside—and a rack filled with floggers, whips, canes and riding crops.

There was a set of cuffs dangling from chains in the ceiling that he'd rigged to a pulley system so he could suspend the lucky subject of his dominant attentions. Earlier in the week Shea had experienced the utter helplessness of being raised so high that only her tiptoes touched the ground. She had panicked for a moment, and had blurted that she needed to be lowered. Yet, when he had complied, she had felt curiously let down and, after a few moments, asked to be raised again.

Now he led her once more to the center of the room and she glanced up at the cuffs, wondering if he was going to suspend her again, hopeful that he was, as she had come to love the feeling of being bound, whether in rope, or leather and chain.

Instead of directing her to lift her arms, however, Liam brought a low, wide padded bench over. "Lie down on the bench on your back, feet flat on the floor."

Shea did as she was told, keenly aware of her freshly shaven pussy, and his promise of a cunt whipping. Liam went to the whip rack and returned a moment later with a short-handled strap made of a thick strip of black leather folded over into a long rectangular loop. "This strap is perfect for delivering a big sting over a small area," he said, cracking it against his thigh for emphasis.

He knelt beside her and ran the cool leather strap over her nipples, which instantly hardened to attention. "I usually bind you for your whippings, but today you will offer me your body, which you have made fully accessible to me. You will lift your ass off the bench, hips arched upward, and you will use your hands to spread your bare cunt for me. I will give you twenty smacks with the strap directly on your cunt. You will hold your position the entire time, keeping yourself spread and open to me. Can you do that, Shea?"

Shea's mouth had gone dry and it was suddenly hard to catch her breath. "I—I don't know, Sir. It's going to hurt."

"Yes." Liam nodded. "You will suffer for me. That pleases me." He stroked his cock beneath the soft denim of his faded jeans, drawing Shea's eyes to his large erection. She moved her gaze up his bare, muscular torso to his handsome face. Her cunt throbbed. She wanted to suffer for him, and the realization both thrilled and frightened her.

"Then it pleases me, Sir," she whispered, heart pounding.

Modesty had no place in a D/s relationship, so he'd told her again and again. She had managed to get more comfortable with her constant nudity, and his scrutiny of every part of her body, even her ass. This was just one more step on the path to full submission, a path she was thrilled to be on, even when the journey scared her.

Liam stood and took a step back, his eyes never leaving her body as he fingered the strap. Shea lifted her hips and reached for her outer labia, pulling them open to fully expose herself. Biting her lip, she squeezed her eyes closed, her body tensing in anticipation of the sting of the flat strap against her sensitive folds.

"Relax," Liam said. Bending down, he stroked her face, his touch warm and comforting. Shea opened her eyes. Liam was smiling encouragingly at her, his expression gentle, though his eyes sparked with a lust that thrilled Shea to her bones. "You can do this," he said. "I know you can. I would never ask more of you than you can give, Shea. Do you believe that?"

Shea nodded. Each time she'd been afraid, he'd led her through the fear, and she'd come out of the experience stronger and more empowered than before, and always eager for more.

Liam nodded as if she'd said these thoughts aloud. "I want you to flow with the experience, rather than resisting it. Think about what you've learned. Let go of that control. Give it to me. Don't anticipate, don't resist. Just *be*."

He stood and moved to the end of the bench. Crouching between her legs, he drew the leather strap over her spread cunt. Shea shivered at the feel of the leather but held her position. "I'll start light," he said, "and increase the intensity slowly. Twenty strokes. You can count for me to help you stay focused. And remember, keep your position or we'll have to start over. Are we clear?"

"Yes, Sir," Shea breathed.

~*~

As he crouched between Shea's long, slender legs, Liam inhaled the delicate scent of her musk. He could see her desire in the swell of her labia. Unable to resist, he bent forward and snaked out his tongue, running it in a line along her soft inner labia and circling the little marble of her clit. Shea mewed like a kitten, and for a second, Liam thought of dropping the strap and licking his girl into a screaming orgasm.

No, he admonished himself. *That will be her reward, and mine, after the strapping.*

He admired the lovely sea-shell perfect curves of her shaven cunt. He had thought of shaving her himself, but had decided he would wait until they were together on a more permanent basis before he broached that particular subject with her.

What a delightful surprise to find she'd done it herself. What a lovely, pure gesture of erotic submission. Not for the first time, he marveled that a person could spend their life completely unaware of their own deep-seated sexual impulses. Though it was years before he'd dared to act upon them, Liam had been aware of his dominant urges and needs since his early teens, or even before that. His favorite games in primary school included the ones where the boys would chase the girls and hold them captive. Nothing had excited him more than the pretending to whip the girls with vines and then locking them into pretend jails made from pieces of fencing and boards he'd cobbled together in his backyard.

It had taken him much longer, however, to understand and accept that his desire to inflict erotic pain and dominant control wasn't at odds with his love and respect of women. He'd kept his erotic fantasies secret, even from the woman he'd married. It had taken a submissive woman named Donna he'd met at a BDSM club to really help him grasp and internalize that erotic sadism and domination had their perfect complement in erotic masochism and submission. If Donna hadn't been thirty years his senior and married to boot, who knows what might have developed between them.

As it was, he had found the woman of his dreams at last on an island in paradise, but now that woman was flying halfway round the world in two days' time. *That's two days you didn't have before you met her. Savor the moment. Enjoy each second as if it were your last.*

He drew the strap over her glistening cunt and she stiffened. He didn't admonish her, but instead brought the strap down lightly against her flesh. "One," she said in a tremulous voice. He slapped her spread cunt again, just as lightly as before. "Two," she said, a shade more forcefully. The third stroke was slightly harder, though only enough to sting just a little. "Three!" The word was expelled with a small gasp.

Liam looked at Shea's face. She was watching him with wide eyes, her chest rising and falling. "Breathe," he reminded her. "You're doing great. I'm going to increase the intensity now. Remember to keep your position and don't lose count."

The fourth stroke landed with a crack. Instead of calling out the number, Shea squealed and brought her hands over her cunt, falling completely out of position, her bottom falling back to the padded bench. Though Liam had expected this at some point, he was surprised it had come so soon. Perhaps she was especially sensitive because of the recent shaving.

"Oh dear," he said. "Out of position so soon. We'll have to start over, you know. Back in position, sub girl. Lift your hips, spread that cunt and offer yourself to me."

Shea bit her lower lip in that charming way she had when she was nervous, but her nipples, Liam noted, jutted hard from her breasts, and the scent of her arousal was like a heady perfume filling the air.

He waited while she lifted her body into the required position and placed her fingers on either side of her perfect cunt.

The fifth stroke was as hard as the fourth, but Shea managed to keep her position as she cried out, "One!"

"Good girl." He smacked her again, moving the strap slightly to catch her at a different angle.

"Two!"

Liam's cock ached. While he enjoyed his sessions with the submissives who paid for training, he never got hard like this with them. He never wanted to yank down his jeans and plunge his cock inside them. Christ, he had never wanted anyone the way he wanted Shea. He should have insisted she refuse the promotion. He should have ordered her to quit her job entirely and assume her rightful place as his full-time sub girl.

Maybe in his twenties he would have done exactly that foolish thing, and thereby guaranteed the loss of her. Shea was too independent, and too heavily invested in her career. He could never ask that of her. If and when that ever happened, it would have to be her idea, and hers alone.

"Three! Four! Five! Oh god, I can't, I can't..."

"You can. You are. You're magnificent." *Smack*.

"Six. Seven. Eight..."

The last few strokes were just whispers of leather against her reddened labia. As she murmured, "Twenty," Liam dropped the strap and leaned eagerly forward, cupping the luscious globes of her ass as he licked and suckled her hot, swollen cunt. She tasted like honey and passion and the Caribbean Sea, and he couldn't get enough of her sweetness, or the shudder of her body, or her mewling cries and breathy request to come.

"Yes," he said, lifting his head just long enough to reply. "Come for me, beautiful girl." As she shuddered and bucked against his mouth, he managed to yank down his jeans and grip his shaft. Lifting himself over her, he guided his cock into her heat. She was wet from his kisses and slick with lust, and it felt as if her cunt were grabbing him and pulling him inside.

Though he'd wanted to prolong it, her sexy, breathy cries and the delicious grip of her hot cunt soon had his balls tightening with an impending orgasm he knew he couldn't fight off. He pulled her against his chest as he exploded inside her, burying his face in her soft, shiny hair until his own spasms subsided.

They lay still for several long moments. He became aware of the ticking of the clock mounted on the wall to keep track during professional sessions. Time was passing. The seconds were flying by. In two short days, she would be gone.

Don't leave me, he wanted to cry. *Not ever. Not for a second.*

"I love you," he said instead. "You are my darling girl."

Chapter 14

Shea stared out the airplane window at the wide expanse of ocean far below. Howard Williams sat next to her in the business class seat, clacking away on his laptop. In his early fifties, he was lean and sparse, with chiseled features and flinty gray eyes. He'd already given Shea a thick file of prospective clients for her to get up to speed on during the flight. Shea had made a half-hearted attempt to comply, but her mind kept drifting inexorably back to Liam.

She had wanted him to come too. She'd even looked into his booking a seat on the flight she and Howard were on, not able to bear the thought of parting from him so soon, but in the end cooler heads had prevailed, mainly Liam's. "It will be better this way, you'll see. Until you get settled, I don't want to distract you with my inimitable presence," he had teased, but in fact he was right.

When she was around Liam, everything else just fell away. Nothing else seemed to matter outside the realm of their love. All she wanted to do was be with him—in his arms, in his bed, kneeling naked at his feet or bound naked and willing to the St. Andrew's Cross in his dungeon, eager to feel the sharp cut of the cane, the thuddy kiss of the flogger, or the warm press of his lips against hers.

"I'll fly over as soon as you send for me," Liam had assured her. "I'll be here waiting, I promise."

She believed him, and took great comfort from his declaration, but still she hated the thought of leaving him, even for a few weeks. And then there was that niggling little emotion tunneling through her thoughts like a worm in an apple—jealousy.

She knew intellectually it wasn't necessary or worthy of her. Though he continued to train submissive women in a context that could only be described as intimate, she understood that Liam was a professional, and there were bounds he would never cross with these women.

The odd thing was Shea had never been a jealous sort of person. She wasn't one of those girlfriends who took offense if her man checked out a good looking woman. She hadn't even been all that concerned with exclusivity, even when things got serious.

But with Liam it was different. For the first time in her life, she felt possessive. She had expressed some of her feelings to Liam, who had said he understood, but assured her there was no need to worry. When he was training, there was nothing sexual or romantic going on. It was just his way of giving back to the BDSM community, a kind of calling to help others connect with that part of themselves. Again, intellectually, Shea admired this, but that didn't stop her from wanting to screen all the applicants. Beautiful young women need not apply.

Trust.

That was what it boiled down to. A matter of trust. So much of submission, she had been learning, was based on trust—not only of your Dom, but of yourself. It was about letting go and trusting the process, and it was harder than anything she'd ever done in her life, but worth the struggle. She was still learning to let go of the iron grip of control she'd held over her emotions ever since she was a little girl trying to fend off and deal with her bullying older brother, Jeff, without the benefit of parents to intervene.

Her mother, an active alcoholic who loved her booze more than her kids, was rarely coherent enough to take notice of, much less protect Shea from Jeff's frequent bouts of aggressive behavior. Her father, a driven man who spent as little time at home as possible, only seemed to recognize his children's existence when they achieved something he valued, like getting good grades, excelling at sports, or graduating at the top of the class. Any appeals to him for protection or support had been met with a shrug and the advice to fight fire with fire, which wasn't much help when you were a six-year-old girl trying to deal with a ten-year-old brother who, she understood in retrospect, had to have felt as angry and impotent as she had.

She had adapted by becoming completely self-sufficient, and keeping her emotions safely hidden away, oftentimes even from herself. This had stead her well in her professional life, but the cost had been huge. She had had no one to turn to, no one who really knew her, because she wouldn't allow it.

But not any longer.

In just the short time they'd been together, Liam had become her safe place.

If she truly trusted Liam, she needed to let go of those unproductive and even harmful jealous feelings. After all, Liam trusted her to travel across the world and spend who knew how many weeks apart. He'd even given her the name of several BDSM clubs he thought she might enjoy visiting, along with the name and email address of a dominant friend of his, Patrick O'Connor, whom he suggested she contact when she was ready to check out the London scene.

"He's been put on notice," Liam had added with a grin, though Shea knew from his tone he was dead serious, "that you belong to me, and if he knows what's good for him, he'll keep his hands off." Shea's typical reaction in any other relationship would have been to bristle and inform Liam that she belonged only to herself, and would make those sorts of decisions on her own. But coming from him, the words had warmed her, making her feel cherished in the best sense of the word.

The loudspeaker clicked on, recalling Shea to the present. "We'll be landing at Heathrow in approximately twenty minutes," the captain said. "Flight attendants, please prepare for landing."

"Take the rest of the day off," Howard said, as if he were planning to go directly to their new offices from the airport. Maybe he was driven enough to do just that. "Your apartment is close to our offices and it's fully furnished. I'll have our driver take you there. In the morning we'll hammer out our game plan and start the interview process to staff up the place." His lips lifted, revealing teeth, and Shea realized he was smiling. "This is quite an opportunity, young lady. I know you've done excellent work for the firm back in Houston, but we're going to have to bust our asses here to make a name for Sutton Investments. Nothing will be handed to us. I trust you're up to the challenge."

Though she believed she was, anxiety suddenly surged through her as she thought about the momentous task ahead of them. Sure, she'd been a success back in Texas, but that was known territory, familiar ground. Jackie had given her carte blanche, while Howard was known as something of a control freak.

Well, she'd signed up for this. It wouldn't do to back out now. *Never let them see you sweat.* Shea took a deep cleansing breath and met Howard's flinty gaze with a confident smile. "You bet," she said. "Bring it on."

~*~

It was Friday night and Shea was almost too tired to eat, but since she'd had nothing since mid morning, she made herself have some dinner. She had bought some Indian take-out food, or take away as they called it in London. After eating enough to quiet her rumbling stomach, she poured herself a glass of wine and settled on the small, uncomfortable couch in her rented flat. It was really just a one-room studio, with kitchen, living room and bedroom separated by partitions, but Shea had barely had time to notice in the two weeks since she'd been in the UK.

Nearly every waking moment had been spent at the office, as she and Howard gave it everything they had. Shea still managed to find time, though just barely, to check in with Liam via Skype, and each time she saw his handsome face on her screen, it felt as if someone had reached into her chest and wrapped a fist around her heart.

The two or three minute visits were woefully inadequate substitutes for actually being with him, but they were better than nothing. Because London was six hours ahead of Houston, when she was finally able to wrap up a day's work at around nine each night, Shea didn't feel it was fair to Skype Liam, though he claimed he kept his laptop open and on the bed beside him, in case she changed her mind.

No matter how many hours she put in, Howard expected more. She hadn't found time to call Liam's friend, Patrick, or time to do much of anything except work and sleep. Though Liam sometimes sent her sexy emails, there had been very little overt D/s interaction between them, since long distance sex didn't appeal to either of them, and more to the point, Shea was just too wiped out at the end of each day to even think about it.

Reaching for her iPad, she opened her personal email, in case Liam had written her a good night message, as he often did. The subject line sent a jolt of excitement through Shea's body.

To: SheaDevon713@gmail.com
From: MasterLiamTx@yahoo.com
Subject: Instructions for my sub girl

Shea my darling,

This Saturday you will go to Marie's Boutique on Oxford Street, where you will find a package waiting in your name. You may try the clothes on in the boutique if you wish, but you may only exchange them for a larger or smaller size. Once back at your flat, you will shower, groom yourself and apply full makeup. You will dress in the items from the boutique, and only those items.

At nine o'clock, my friend Patrick O'Connor will pick you up. He will be taking you to a club called Satin & Chains. He will be acting as my surrogate. You will obey him as you would obey me. You may decide, at your discretion, if you wish to participate in a public scene with him. If you do, I know you will make me very proud.

Have fun. I love you. I miss you. See you soon, my love.

Love, Liam

"See you soon, my love," Shea murmured aloud, momentarily distracted by this declaration. They had begun discussing when he should come to the UK, but so far Shea hadn't been able to commit to a date. She still hadn't been able to come up for air at the office. Liam had said he would come to London the second she was ready to see him, even move back to the UK if that was what she wanted, but what kind of life would he have, with her working even longer hours than she had back in the States? How could she ask him to give up the life he'd made for himself in Texas?

Though she was used to hard work, Howard took the concept to whole new levels. She sometimes thought the guy must sleep at the office—no matter how early she arrived or how late she left, he was always there. Once upon a time she wouldn't have minded, but since she'd met Liam, her sense of what was important—really important—had changed.

For the first time in her professional life, she wondered if she'd made the right decision. Now that the excitement of being tapped for such an important position had started to fade, she had even begun to question if maybe the high-pressure, high-stakes career she had chosen came at too high a cost. Doing her job and doing it well was no longer the be-all and end-all of her existence, and the realization was disconcerting.

Despite Howard's iron hand of control, Shea still loved what she did. Yet, while it was exciting to be in a new country and a new environment, she missed some of the comforts of home, and its familiarity. She missed not being able to find some of the foods she liked at the local small and wholly unsatisfactory grocery store that was always closed when she got home in the evenings. She missed the freedom of owning a car, instead having to rely on the tube and taxis, since no way was she going to try driving on the wrong side of the road. She tried not to be annoyed when asked to repeat herself because of her apparently incomprehensible accent, and barely managed to choke down the instant brown powder in tepid water that passed for coffee in so many of the offices she visited.

Mainly, she missed Liam.

She ached for his touch, his conversation, his kiss, his whip and his ropes, but the emptiness in her heart went deeper than that. She missed the profound peace she'd found with Liam, and both the thrill and happiness she'd experienced in his arms.

With a sigh she poured herself another glass of wine and reread Liam's email, this time focusing on the body of the letter. Did he really expect her to get herself to some boutique and blindly accept whatever outfit it was he'd chosen for her? Did he really think she'd go to some BDSM club with a man she had never met and engage in a public scene with him? Who the hell did Liam think he was?

"Your Dom," she said aloud into the empty room. "That's who."

Patrick O'Connor turned out to be thirty-four, though his prematurely gray hair had made Shea think at first that he was older. His face, while not classically handsome, was distinguished, with strong lines, deep-set blue eyes and a long, aquiline nose.

When Shea came down to the main lobby of her building to greet him, he swept her with such an appraising gaze that she blushed. Tall and lean, he was dressed in black leather pants, black boots and a black leather vest over a white button-down shirt that was opened to his breastbone, revealing the head of a black and blue tattooed snake curling up from his left pec.

Shea wasn't used to wearing the sort of clothes Liam had chosen for her, though she had to admit she looked pretty good in the outfit, if high class call girl was the look you were going for. Liam had selected a black lace sheath dress that hugged her curves, the hem falling several inches above her knees. It had a sharp sweetheart neckline that showed plenty of cleavage, and a skin-baring back that didn't allow for a bra. Underneath it were the silky, sheer stockings and satin garter belt he had instructed her to wear, her feet tucked into black platform mules that were several inches higher than anything she owned, but surprisingly comfortable. She wore no panties, again at Liam's dictate.

When she had modeled the outfit for Liam on Skype, his enthusiastic response had made her laugh with pleasure. "It's not what you're used to, is it, Shea?" he had asked as he drank her in with his eyes.

"No way," she'd agreed. "But I have to admit, I kind of like it."

"I kind of love it," he'd responded with a grin. Then his look had changed, and even from across the ocean, she had felt his dominant pull, and her yielding response. "Turn around," he had said, his voice deepening. Shea had turned her back to the laptop screen.

"Bend over and lift your skirt."

She had done so, spreading her legs so her Dom could view her bare ass and smooth pussy. "Jesus, Shea," Liam had sighed. "You are sheer perfection. Stand up and turn around. I need to kiss you."

Kissing the computer screen was, of course, highly unsatisfactory. "Soon," Shea had whispered to the blank screen once Liam had logged off. But when? How?

As they headed outside, Patrick surprised Shea by opening the back door of the waiting car, which made her think for a moment he expected her to sit alone back there while he drove. When Patrick scooted in beside her, she saw there was a driver already at the wheel.

As the driver navigated the London streets, Patrick and Shea made small talk about how Shea was getting on in London, and what Liam was like in high school, which was where Patrick and Liam had met. Patrick was pleasant and easygoing, and Shea relaxed.

"Liam's told me a bit about you," Patrick eventually said. "A newbie to BDSM—innocent as a lamb. I hope you're up to the lion's den into which I'm going to take you, my dear."

Shea's natural competitive instinct kicked in. "Not so innocent as all that. I can handle myself, thank you."

Patrick laughed. "I'm sure you can, Shea. I look forward to finding out firsthand."

They drove along in silence for a while, Shea now nervous as a cat. Patrick's cell phone, or mobile as they called them in the UK, buzzed repeatedly and he kept pulling it from his jacket, executing rapid fire responses with his thumbs. Shea thought this was a little rude, but Liam had mentioned Patrick was a doctor, so maybe he was on call or something.

The car finally rolled to a stop in front of a large, unprepossessing building located on Tinworth Street near the Vauxhall Station. "Here we are, then," Patrick said. Climbing out of the car, he held open the door for Shea and then leaned into the front passenger window to murmur something to the driver. Reaching into the front seat, he pulled out what Shea saw was a small duffel bag, which he slung over his shoulder as he watched the car ease away from the curb and melt back into the traffic.

Shea's mouth was dry. She tugged discreetly at the short hem of her dress and drew in a deep, calming breath. They stood before a black door with a large brass knocker at its center. Shea turned to Patrick. "This is it? How would anyone even know there was a club here?"

"It's a private club—by invitation only. You won't find the usual wankers and tourists gawking about here. This place is for people who are seriously into the scene. Anything goes, as long as you observe the three S's."

"The three S's?"

"Safe, sane and consensual." Patrick lifted the brass knocker and let it fall with a rap against the door.

After a few seconds, a voice emanated from a small intercom to the side of the door. "May I help you?"

"Patrick O'Connor and guest," Patrick said. After another few seconds there was a buzzing sound and then a click. Patrick reached for the knob and pulled the door open to reveal a narrow flight of concrete steps that led downward.

Not used to walking in the mules, Shea was grateful for the handrails on either side of the stairs, and for Patrick's firm hand on her shoulder as he walked behind her. There was another door at the bottom of the stairs, and this was pulled open just as they arrived by a tall dark-skinned man who wore a thick chain around his neck. He was naked, save for a cream-colored satin apron that barely covered his genitals. He stepped back with a dip of his head.

"Welcome, Master Patrick," he said in a deep voice. Nodding toward Shea, he added, "Mistress."

"Good evening, Thomas. This is Shea," Patrick said. "She is no Mistress. She is my sub for the evening." Turning to Shea, he said, "Isn't that right, Shea?"

Gone was the good-humored, easygoing man she had been talking with on the drive to the club. She could feel power radiating from him like a magnetic field. Patrick was boring into her with those deep-set eyes, clearly waiting for a response.

Shea started to deny what he'd said, but then remembered Liam's instructions. "Yes, Sir," she managed.

Thomas reached for something from the table by the door and held it out toward Patrick, who took it. Patrick turned to Shea, holding up a chain collar similar to the one Thomas was wearing. "All slaves and subs wear collars while in the club. Kneel and lift your hair so I can place this around your neck."

Again the urge to refuse surfaced, but Shea swallowed her resistance. Patrick was Liam's surrogate for the night. She lowered herself carefully to the thickly piled carpet and bent her head, lifting her hair as Patrick clipped the heavy, cold chain around her neck. Once it was in place, Patrick held out his hand to help her stand, and Shea allowed him to pull her upright.

Shea touched the cold chain at her throat as they entered the room, reminded suddenly of the leather collar Liam had produced back at the island, and the words he had said then, words she had since come to truly understand and embrace. "The collar symbolizes possession," he had said. "It represents your surrender of control, your willingness to submit." A sudden, overwhelming desire to be once more in Liam's arms washed over her with such force that she nearly fell to her knees.

"Are you all right?" Patrick's arm was suddenly around her shoulders, his expression concerned as he gazed down at her.

"Oh," Shea replied, embarrassed. "It was—just my shoes. I'm not used to them."

She took in the space, which was dimly lit by gold metal sconces set at intervals along walls painted a deep burgundy red. There were several clusters of small tables around a long bar set against one wall, many of them occupied. Half a dozen naked men and women dressed like Thomas in chain collars, satin aprons and nothing else were weaving among the tables with trays of drinks.

Shea tried to imagine herself walking nearly naked through a room of strangers and failed. Yet who would have imagined just a month ago that she would find herself in an underground London BDSM club on the arm of a compelling stranger whom she'd promised her lover she would obey as if he were her Dom?

Seize the moment, she reminded herself. She hadn't gotten as far as she had in her life by shrinking from challenges. She wasn't about to start now. *Just stay cool. Act like you've been to one of these places before. Don't be the gawking Yank Patrick thinks you are.*

To the right of the bar was an archway that led into another room that clearly was the dungeon. As they moved toward it, Shea could see the room was partitioned into various stations, each of which contained a piece of BDSM equipment, some of which Shea recognized, like the St. Andrew's Cross, a suspension rack, and a set of stocks, the latter of which was occupied by a rather large and completely naked woman.

Shea was relieved when Patrick veered away from the archway, leading her instead toward the bar. Though she wanted to play, she wasn't quite ready. As they approached, Shea saw a naked man with a black hood over his head kneeling on all fours beside one of the tables. The woman sitting beside him had propped her high-heel-clad feet on his back and every few seconds she would snap a long riding crop against his ass, though she seemed otherwise to ignore him, instead focusing on the fully-clothed man at her table.

Patrick pulled out a chair at an empty table, and Shea sank into it, relieved she hadn't been directed to get on all fours. A striking young woman with improbably red hair and small, high breasts with gold hoops through the nipples appeared beside the table dressed in the club's uniform of satin and chains.

"Good evening, Master Patrick," she said. Clearly, this guy was a regular. The serving girl completely ignored Shea. "What can I get you this evening?"

"I'll have a glass of Cabernet. My sub will have a glass of orange juice."

Shea could have used a couple of shots of rum in that orange juice, but she bit her lip instead of protesting. Liam had taught her that alcohol and BDSM play didn't mix, especially between people who didn't know each other all that well. Was Patrick's glass of wine an indication that he was only there to watch? More to the point, was his choice for her beverage an indication that he expected more from her?

Shea didn't voice her questions, having learned in business that sometimes it was best to say nothing, especially when you were on unsteady ground. She would wait and see what Patrick had in mind for her. Liam had instructed her to obey Patrick as she would himself, but he'd also said it was her decision whether or not she engaged in a public scene with him.

A couple came by the table and Patrick invited them to sit. Introductions were made and small talk ensued. Shea had a hard time focusing on the conversation. What she really wanted to do was go check out the dungeon, but she didn't want to appear rude. Maybe Patrick was just making sure she was comfortable first. It was thoughtful of him, she told herself.

The couple finally meandered away. The wait-slave, if that's what she was called, reappeared and this time Patrick ordered water for them both, again without consulting Shea on the matter. While they were waiting for their drinks, Patrick pulled out his phone once more and glanced expectantly at it. He apparently didn't see what he was looking for, and he slipped it back into his jacket.

Finally he stood and said, "Let's go check out some of the action."

This was more like it.

As they entered the archway, Shea saw a big metal cage with ropes hanging from the bars. Inside it were three women who appeared to be walking on the backs of two naked men. The women were gripping the ropes as they walked over the men with wicked-looking spiked heels. The men were moaning.

Forgetting her admonition to herself to be cool, Shea blurted, "Oh my god, that has to hurt like hell!"

Following her gaze, Patrick smiled. "That's the idea. It's called trampling, and for some it's a very erotic experience indeed." As they watched, one of the men twisted back his head and opened his mouth. One of the women slipped the toe of her pointy shoe between his lips and he closed his eyes, his expression one of pure ecstasy.

They watched a few whipping scenes, and two women who were dripping candle wax directly on the cock and balls of a man lying on the ground between them. A woman in a black bustier and thigh high stockings was suspended from the ceiling by a series of ropes secured to cuffs at her wrists, ankles, thighs and waist. A man stood beneath her with a long, scary-looking single tail whip in his hands. The sonic crack as the tip made contact caused Shea to wince and turned away.

Patrick's pocket began to buzz again and, with a glance at her, he pulled it out and stared down at the screen with a frown. "You're getting a lot of texts," Shea said, barely bothering to hide her annoyance at this point. "Is everything okay?"

Patrick looked up quickly as he slipped the phone back into his jacket. "Oh, sorry. Yes, everything is fine. Just a little change of plans."

What the heck? Was he going to bale on her when they'd only just arrived? What was going on? "Change of plans? Do you have to leave or something?"

"No, no. Not at all. Everything's fine. Sorry. It's all good. Come back to the table. I want to show you something." Shea followed Patrick back to their table, wondering what was going on. Once they were seated, Patrick reached down and unzipped the duffel bag he'd brought. He pulled something out and set it on the table between them.

It was a flogger with a burnished metal handle with easily two dozen black leather straps protruding from it. "Oh." The word was pulled from Shea before she could stop it. Though it wasn't Liam's black-handled flogger with the impossibly soft suede tresses that could caress or sting, depending on his delivery, just the sight of the implement made something soften and open inside Shea, and the skin on her back and ass began to tingle.

She looked over at Patrick, who was regarding her with hooded eyes, one side of his mouth lifted in a half smile. "Liam tells me you are a natural submissive, Shea. He told me how far you've come in just the short time he's been working with you."

Shea smiled, his words at once warming her and making her sad. She felt the lack of Liam even more in that moment, if that was possible. Blinking back tears, she turned her gaze once more to the beautiful flogger.

"Go on," Patrick said, his smile curving into a full grin. "You may touch it."

Unable to resist, Shea stroked the leather strands, an involuntary shudder moving through her body. She lifted the flogger, bringing her face close to the leather and inhaling deeply, barely able to suppress a moan.

"You were born for the whip. It's written all over you."

She knew it was Patrick speaking, but for some reason her brain processed it as Liam, so much so that she was startled for a split second when she looked up and found not Liam's liquid, loving gaze, but Patrick's blue-eyed stare. "I would be honored to test your submissive grace in handling a public flogging. Do I have your permission, sub girl?"

Shea swallowed hard, struggling to hear his words over her own heartbeat suddenly pounding in her ears. She glanced around the room, which was filled with people in various states of undress, none of whom seemed the least bit self conscious. Would Patrick expect her to get naked? Did she have the nerve?

Her eye was drawn back to the dungeon, where hardcore torture scenes were going on in every corner. She knew she couldn't handle anything so intense, not unless Liam were the one to guide her, and not in a public venue.

But a sensual flogging with that gorgeous flogger, wielded by a man who knew what he was doing, by a man Liam himself had selected? Shea's nipples were straining against the lacy fabric of her dress and she could feel the moistness between her legs. She lifted the glass of water to her lips and then set it quickly down again, wondering if Patrick had seen that her hand was shaking.

She stroked the strands of the flogger. How she longed for the kiss of leather against her skin. She ached for the sharp, perfect stroke of the flogger's leather fingers, and the way they carried her to an altered state of consciousness that was as pure and perfect as the infinite blue waters surrounding their secret island in paradise.

She looked up, meeting Patrick's eye, wondering if he could see the longing in her face. Lifting a hand, she touched the chain at her throat. "Yes, Sir," she said in a low voice. "Please."

Chapter 15

Patrick led Shea through the archway once more. They went all the way to the back wall of the large space, stopping in front of a semi-circular platform raised a few feet above the ground. Long chains hung from the beamed ceiling overhead. Patrick stepped up onto the platform, duffel bag over his shoulder. Turning, he held out a hand for Shea to join him.

She glanced nervously around the crowded dungeon, wishing he'd chosen something a little more private than this raised dais with no sheltering partition around it. Reminding herself she was Shea Devon, she took his hand and allowed herself to be hoisted up.

"Take off your shoes," Patrick instructed, for which Shea was grateful. She slipped out of the mules and set them on the edge of the platform while Patrick pulled the flogger and something else from the bag. He held up a pair of black leather wrists cuffs with clips attached. "Hold out your wrists," he said.

Shea did as she was told, glad to see her hands were steady, though her heart was pounding. Patrick secured a soft leather cuff around each wrist. Already a few people had come to stand around the platform. Shea could feel their eyes boring curiously into her.

She heard someone whisper loudly, asking if she was a newbie.

"Take off your dress," Patrick said.

Shea stiffened. "Excuse me?"

"You didn't hear me? I said, take off your dress. You may leave on your under things."

"I'm not wearing…That is, I don't…" She wrapped her arms protectively around herself, though in light of where they were, she knew she was being silly.

Apparently Patrick agreed. "Shea, look around you. This is hardly a place to be concerned about baring your body. Be proud of who and what you are. I can't flog you properly with all that lace in the way. And I'd ruin the dress. You don't want to go home in tatters, do you?"

"Well, no, but—"

"Then take off the dress. Now."

Shea sucked in a breath. There were now easily ten people clustered around the platform, all of them listening to the exchange. Liam's words came back to her: *You will obey him as you would obey me.* Would Liam have asked her to strip in front of strangers? Did it matter? Patrick was Liam's surrogate for tonight. Shea had agreed to this. She wasn't going to back out now.

Glancing nervously once more at the onlookers, Shea reached for her left strap and pulled it down her shoulder. "Keep your eyes on me," Patrick said, and Shea was grateful for this command. She shimmied out of the dress, slipped it down her legs and stepped out of it. An appreciative murmur moved through the small crowd around them and other people began moving toward the dais. Patrick held out his hand and she let him take the dress, which he handed down to a woman standing below them. Shea stood in stockings and garters, heat flaming over her face and chest, but she held her head high. She was Shea Devon. She could do this.

"Turn to face the back wall and lift your arms against the chains," Patrick said, and Shea turned as directed. He appeared in front of her and she focused on his face as he reached up to clip her cuffs to the chains. The snug feel of the cuffs and the taut pull of the chains had their effect on Shea. She eased into that dark, delicious space where she welcomed erotic pain. Closing her eyes, she could almost hear the sound of the waves and feel the warmth of the soft sand beneath bare feet. She could almost feel Liam's fingers stroking her cheek as he leaned close to whisper something to her.

"What's your safeword?" Patrick's voice snapped Shea out of her daydream and she opened her eyes, focusing on the man's long, thin face.

"Red light," she replied, her heart now kicking into high gear.

Patrick offered a rather mocking grin. "How original," he said drily.

Shea started to defend her choice, but he put a finger to her lips. "Just teasing. As of this moment, you will not speak, unless asked a direct question, or, of course, unless you need to use your safeword." He stepped to stand beside her, and in a louder voice, he continued, "Forget where you are. There is no one here but you and me. Your focus is to be entirely on the flogger and the sensations it creates. Are you ready, sub girl?"

Shea swallowed hard. If only it were Liam standing in front of her, instead of this stranger. If only Liam and she were alone on the island together, with all the time in the world. She gripped the chains above her cuffs and shifted her legs a little, planting her feet firmly on the smooth wood of the platform.

Make me proud.

Liam's voice echoed in her mind so clearly that for one startled second she thought he was there. But no, he was thousands of miles away, across an ocean. Nevertheless, she would make him proud. She would show Patrick and all those gawkers standing beneath her waiting for a show that she was just as good a sub as anyone there. She could take whatever this guy meted out.

"Yes, Sir," she said resolutely. "I'm ready."

He moved behind her, the flogger in his hand. The first stroke landed harder than she expected, though it was nothing she couldn't handle. He focused on her ass for a while, bringing the leather down in a crisscrossing pattern over her cheeks. When he moved up to her back, Shea began to pant in an effort not to cry out. Where Liam modulated the intensity based on where the flogger landed, Patrick seemed to be hitting her just as hard on her back and shoulders as he had on her ass.

Shea closed her eyes, trying to ease herself into that serene, perfect place where Liam took her but it was no good. *Too soon*, she told herself. *Just flow with the pain. You'll get there.* One particularly hard blow across both shoulders made her yelp and jerk instinctively away.

"Stay still," Patrick barked. He struck her again in the same spot, and again she yelped, though she managed not to dance away, compensating instead by gripping hard on the chains over her wrists.

The floggers swished and stung over her back, her ass and her thighs, until her skin felt like it was on fire. Still he struck her, again and again and again, until sweat was trickling down her sides and glistening between her breasts. She shook away her hair and tried to wipe her damp forehead against her shoulder but couldn't manage it from her position.

On and on the leather rained down against her burning skin. Why hadn't the sensation shifted by now, as it always had with Liam, into something beyond pain, something above suffering? Why wasn't she flying?

Because he's not Liam.

Close your eyes.

Focus on Liam.

She closed her eyes, trying to conjure the sea, the sand, the smell of salt in the air, Liam's handsome face and kind eyes. The flogger sliced across her back. She began to tremble. It was no good. She couldn't do it. It hurt too much.

Oh, it hurt, it hurt, it hurt.

"Spread your legs."

Patrick's command gave her something to focus on other than the pain. She obeyed, though doing so pulled the cuffs tight against her wrists. The sudden cut of the leather strands coming from behind and catching her spread cunt took her breath away. The second stroke brought it back, and she screamed.

"No!" she cried as the flogger struck again, sending a dozen tiny bee stings across her tender sex. She slammed her legs together and twisted back her head.

"Face forward," Patrick said sternly. "This is where the grace comes in. This is where you show me your obedience and your courage." He struck her ass hard, the leather slapping against her skin with the force of a paddle.

Her entire body was shaking and a bead of sweat rolled into her eye. Blinking back tears, she was suddenly hyper-aware of the crowd below her. Patrick moved close behind her, his voice soft in her ear. "We can stop, Shea. We can stop now. Just say the words."

Red light.

She only had to say those two little words, and all this would be over. Patrick would stop flaying her alive. He would let her down. She could pull on her clothes and stop the gawkers from staring up at her. She could wash her face. She could go back to her flat and shower until the hot water ran out.

Liam would forgive her. He would understand. She clenched the chains, frowning. To stop now was to quit. To quit before the miracle, as Jackie liked to say. Shea was no quitter. Shea finished what she started, come hell or high water. This wasn't so bad. She had just panicked for a moment, taken by surprise by the cunt whipping. She could do this. She *would* do it. For Liam, but more importantly, for herself.

"No," she replied, her voice tremulous but resolute. "I can do this. I can handle it."

"Good girl."

Liam used to say that to her. Shea smiled.

The flogger struck her ass, the tips curling painfully around her hips. Shea blew out a breath and thrust her ass back to meet the strokes. She could hear Patrick's soft, approving chuckle. He struck her again, this time angling the whip so the tips bit into the tender skin of her inner thighs. She hissed her pain but somehow managed to maintain her position, feet flat on the floor.

The flogger moved from her ass to her back to her shoulders to her thighs without any predictable rhythm, each cut as painful as the last. Each time she thought she might be slipping at last into that peaceful, perfect space Liam seemed so effortlessly to bring her to, something would throw her out of sync—a stroke landing too hard, someone grunting below her, something just not right.

You can do it, she urged herself, trying not to grit her teeth or clench her jaw. She was resisting, but she didn't know how to stop. She needed Liam. He would know how to gentle her, to soothe her, to lead her where she so desperately longed to go.

She tried to focus on her breathing. In…and out. In…and out. Then something was nudging insistently at her ankle and Patrick said, "Spread your legs. I'm going to whip your cunt again. You will not move. You will not resist."

His words and their import yanked her once more out of her internal rhythm. She could feel a muscle jumping in her jaw and her pulse throbbing in her throat. Using the last of her will, she forced her legs to spread, leaning heavily against the chains to support herself.

The whip cut like knives between her legs and she cried out in pain. It took every ounce of self-control not to slam her legs together. *I can't, I can't, I can't.* She couldn't stop the words that were chanting inside her head. It was hard to think straight. She needed to be let down. This wasn't working. She couldn't do it.

She became aware that Patrick had stopped the flogging for a moment, thank god. The crowd behind her was murmuring excitedly. She could hear Patrick shifting and thumping on the platform for some reason. She started to twist around, to tell him it was time to stop, but he snapped, "Head forward. Keep your position," with such force that she was startled into obeying. She turned to face the wall once more, trying to muster her strength and clear her muddled brain.

The flogging began again, this time the rhythm steady against her ass, first just kissing the skin, only slowly increasing in intensity. This was better. *Thank you, Patrick* she wanted to say, but instead she just focused on the silky sting, letting the image of Liam move through her mind.

The flogger moved now down to her thighs and then swept in a sensual dance over her back and shoulders. Yes. Yes, this was it. This was what she had needed, not the herky-jerky delivery from before. Her head fell back as the whip caressed her with its leather kiss. Her skin felt warm, her heartbeat slowing, her breath easing, her mouth falling open. The flogger was landing as hard as before, or harder, but the miracle had happened. The pain had transmuted, melting and twisting with strands of deep, abiding pleasure and consuming peace.

She could no longer hear the murmur of the crowd. There was only her breathing, her heartbeat and the sensual slap and swish of the flogger moving over her skin like a lover's hands. She could see Liam so clearly in her mind's eye. He was with her. She could even smell his Bay Rum cologne.

"Liam," she whispered, unable to stop the word that tumbled from her lips. "Liam," she said louder.

"Yes, my darling. I'm here."

Chapter 16

Time seemed to stop as reality shifted like bits of glass and stone in a kaleidoscope, falling into a pattern that Shea couldn't comprehend with her mind, though her heart already knew. The cuffs were released from her wrists and as she sagged down, strong arms lifted her into an embrace that felt like home. Shea focused on the warm, crinkling eyes and the curve of her lover's smile.

"Liam," she breathed incredulously. "You're here."

"I am," Liam agreed. Still holding her in his arms, Liam stepped down off the platform. The crowd around them parted, and Liam carried Shea through a door at the back of the dungeon into a softly-lit room with several sofas and chairs set against the walls.

He settled onto a deep, plush sofa, Shea still cradled in his arms. With a languorous sigh, Shea let her eyes flutter closed, wondering if perhaps she had fallen into a dream. Liam's soft lips kissed her eyelids, her nose, her chin and her mouth. Soothing ambient music floated through the small room, and above it she heard the murmuring of men, though she didn't try to decipher the words. It might have been seconds or it might have been minutes as Shea drifted in peaceful serenity.

When she eventually opened her eyes, Liam was still there—he was no dream. Shea smiled up at him and he smiled back. "Hey there. You back from the heavens?"

Shea nodded and shifted on Liam's lap. He helped her to sit upright and then draped a red silk robe over her shoulders. Shea pulled it gratefully over her body, suddenly aware of her naked state as she saw Patrick perched on a nearby chair, grinning like a Cheshire cat.

As she looked at Liam's friend, sudden understanding dawned. "So that's why you kept texting all night and acting so strange," she accused, though she was laughing. "You two cooked this whole thing up."

"Guilty as charged." Patrick raised his hands as if in surrender. "I was afraid this bloke wouldn't show. He was forty minutes late as it was."

"Traffic was so bad I thought I was back in Houston," Liam explained, shaking his head. "I even offered the cabbie double the fare to get me here faster, but unfortunately his car didn't have wings."

A naked slave girl appeared at the door of the room, a tray in her hands. On it was a large glass of water, along with three champagne flutes and a bottle of champagne. Patrick stood and took the tray, thanking the girl, who curtsied prettily and slipped out of the room

Patrick handed Shea the glass of water. She took it and drank deeply, the cold, clear water working like a magic elixir to revive her. Once she had finished the glass, Liam took it from her while Patrick popped the cork of the champagne bottle.

As Patrick poured, Shea turned to Liam. "I don't get it. You were talking to me on Skype just this afternoon. How did you get to London so fast from Texas?"

"I was actually at the gate, ready to board when we Skyped. I was hiding in a corner so no one else would see my tablet. I was afraid you were going to notice the sounds of the airport."

"She only had eyes and ears for you," Patrick quipped. He handed a glass to each of them and then lifted his own. "A toast," he said, "to true love." The three of them clinked their glasses. Shea sipped at the bubbly wine, still trying to take it all in.

Patrick shook his head. "Shea, I don't know what you've done to this bloke, but you should know, Liam and I have been friends for over twenty years, and this is the first time I've ever seen that goofy expression on his face." Turning to Liam, he added with a grin, "You've got it bad, my friend."

Liam laughed as he put his arm around Shea and pulled her close. "Good, you mean. I've got it good."

~*~

Shea unlocked the door to her flat and preceded Liam inside. All the patience Liam had brought to bear over the past two hours burned away now that they were alone at last.

Kicking the door closed, Liam grabbed Shea's shoulders and pushed her against the wall. Desperate for her, he took her face in his hands, his mouth crushing hers. As he kissed her, he reached into the low cut top of her dress and pulled her bare breasts free. Dipping his head, he caught one of her nipples between his teeth and tugged.

Shea moaned, her nipple hardening to a round pebble against his tongue. Liam's cock throbbed, his balls tight with need. His mouth still at her breast, he reached for the hem of her short dress, lifting it high to expose her naked body from the waist down.

He cupped her smooth mons, his fingers drawn to the heat between her legs. He pressed his palm lightly against her clit as he slid two fingers inside her. Shea shuddered and moaned against his mouth. He stroked and teased her until she began to tremble.

"Oh god," she breathed, her voice guttural and ragged. "I have to, I need to…"

"Do it. Come for me." He ground his palm against her clit as he moved his fingers inside her. Shea began to buck against his hand, her entire body shaking.

When he couldn't wait another second, Liam yanked at his zipper and pushed his jeans and underwear down his thighs. Reaching around the beautiful girl, he gripped her ass and lifted her onto his shaft. Shea wrapped her legs around his waist and Liam had to restrain himself to keep from slamming savagely into her.

He pinned her against the wall as he fucked her. Her breath came in staccato gasps as he thrust inside her. Though it had only been weeks, it felt like a lifetime since he'd made love to her. His body, heart and soul had been in a kind of suspended animation, brought back to life by the woman in his arms.

All too soon an orgasm slammed through him, hurling him against Shea as he exploded with such intensity it left him nearly senseless. He held Shea in his arms, using the wall to support them both until he remembered how to breathe, how to think, how to move.

Much later, they lay together in bed, Shea resting her check against Liam's chest as she slept. Still on Texas time, Liam was awake, though he felt relaxed and peaceful now that Shea was once more in his arms. Dipping his head, he kissed Shea's hair.

She stirred and lifted her head, her eyes opening sleepily to regard him.

"I'm sorry, I didn't mean to wake you," Liam said.

"It's okay. I don't want to sleep while you're here."

"God, I've missed you," Liam said.

"Me too you."

Flashing a sudden mischievous grin, Shea slipped out of his grasp and slid down beneath the covers. Liam moaned with pleasure when he felt her soft, warm lips wrapping around his rapidly rising shaft.

Shea licked and suckled him, her long, slender fingers stroking and cupping his balls. Liam reached for her, entwining his fingers in her soft, silky hair as she worshipped his cock. All too soon, his body went rigid, and the force of his orgasm momentarily rendered him deaf, mute and blind.

He wanted to take Shea into his arms. To kiss her, to make love to her, to whisper all the words of love and longing he'd saved for her. But all he managed was to lift his arm as she sidled back up to snuggle against his chest. Sleep came up around him like high tide.

The weekend leaped forward like a film made using time-lapse photography. It was Monday morning already, and the clock beside the bed said six fifteen. Shea was bustling around the bedroom. "Come back to bed," Liam demanded.

"I wish I could," Shea replied with a rueful grin. "We have an eight o'clock meeting with some very big deal potential clients. Howard's expecting me to do the presentation. I was planning on using yesterday to prepare, so I'm really under the gun here." She turned toward him, fiddling with an earring at her earlobe. "I'm sorry, Liam. I'll be back as soon as I can, I promise."

Liam made himself smile, though he already felt her lack. "It's okay. I understand. I'll just be a bum today. We'll go out to dinner this evening."

Shea grabbed a silk scarf and draped it artfully around her neck while stepping into pointy-toed shoes. Turning to face him, she fixed Liam with such a woebegone expression he was afraid for a second she was going to burst into tears. In a moment she was across the room. Dropping to the bed beside him, she wrapped her arms around his neck and kissed him. "Oh, Liam," she said plaintively, "I don't know what to do. I don't want to leave you. Not even for a second."

"And I don't want you to go, but I understand you have obligations, sweetheart. Maybe you can arrange for a few days off while I'm here?"

Shea nodded. "Yes. Definitely." She glanced down at the small gold watch on her wrist. "Oh, shit. I do have to go." She stood, looking lovely and professional in her elegant business suit. Bending down, she gave him one last kiss on the lips. "I'll check in later. Love you!" Grabbing her purse and briefcase, she whirled out of the flat.

At five that evening, Liam texted Shea. *Seven o'clock reservations at Ceviche work for you?*

After a few minutes, she texted back, *Still in tricky negotiations. But should be okay for tonight.*

At six thirty, he texted again. *Still on for seven? You want to meet there?*

She eventually responded. *Deal nearly in the bag. Seven thirty?*

Liam hailed a taxi and made it to the restaurant a few minutes past their agreed upon time. A check with the maitre d' confirmed Shea hadn't yet arrived. Liam allowed himself to be led to their table, where he pulled out his phone and shot another text to Shea, trying not to be annoyed. After all, he was the one who had just shown up unannounced.

Liam was on his second beer when, at eight o'clock, a breathless, harried Shea appeared at the door of the restaurant, her briefcase in tow. When she was seated across from him, she pushed her hair from her face and offered Liam a wan smile. "I'm so sorry, Liam. I tried to get out sooner. The new associate we hired called in sick this morning and I had to put out a few fires in addition to what was already on the schedule. As it was I walked out while Howard was still running some numbers. He didn't say anything, but from his expression you would have thought I was leaving at noon." She laughed as she said this, but Liam could see she was exhausted.

He reached out and put his hand over hers. "I ordered you some wine." He pushed the glass toward her. "As your Dom, I order you to think only about us for the rest of the night."

He was relieved when Shea laughed and reached for the wineglass. She took a long drink and set it down with a sigh. "I feel awful that you're here and I have to be at work."

"Did you manage to clear your schedule a bit?" Liam asked, keeping his tone casual. When Shea nodded, he let out the breath he hadn't realized he'd been holding.

"I can't get out of the next few days, but I'm going to take off Thursday and Friday so we can spend the end of the week together with no distractions. When I told Howard, I honestly thought he was going have an epileptic fit, the way his eyes bulged and his face turned all red," she said with a grin. "He doesn't really get the concept of time off, since he never takes any, you see. I don't think he's used to anyone who works under him ever crossing him, but what could he say? I've already logged in enough comp time to take a full week off. Just because he has no life outside of work, doesn't mean I'm in the same boat."

Liam shook his head admiringly. "I am so proud of you, Shea, and grateful too, since now I won't have to execute the kidnap plan I had in mind." He grinned, but then sobered. "Seriously, I know how much this new job means to you and how important it is to put your best foot forward. I really appreciate your finding the time for me—for *us*.

Shea smiled, her eyes sparkling. "You know," she mused, shaking her head, "I used to be Howard—we were cut from the same cloth, with no life except work." She sighed happily. "But since I met you, I'm finally getting it that there's more—way more—to life than work. It's about balance. I've spent my life out of balance—out of sync, and I didn't even know it. But all that's changing now. It has changed. I'm not the woman I was. You've shown me there's a new way, a better way, to be." She frowned, a small worry pucker appearing between her eyebrows. "Now I just have to figure out what the heck to do about it."

Chapter 17

"You're talking too fast, Shea. Take a deep breath, slow down and say it again," Jackie said into the phone.

Shea's heart was still beating a mile a minute after her confrontation with Howard. "I think I might have just been fired."

"What? What's going on?" Jackie said in a concerned tone.

"I had made arrangements to take tomorrow and Friday off because I have a friend in town. Howard didn't like it, but he couldn't really say anything since we've both been working pretty much around the clock since we got here. But then this morning Howard informed me that he was rescinding permission for time off. Rescinding, that's what he said, looking down his nose at me the way he does."

"Why did he do that?"

"Because this company we're working with had a change in their schedule, and he wants me to work through the week and into the weekend to make sure everything's good to go. The thing is, he doesn't even really need me there. We could close the deal today. When I explained that I had plans that couldn't be changed, he said all plans could be changed, and work came first."

"And you said...?"

Shea gave a short, nervous laugh. "I kind of lost my temper. I said maybe it did for him, but some of us actually had a life beyond work, and my plans could not be changed."

Jackie burst out laughing, her guffaws echoing through the phone. "Okay, who is this really, and what have you done with Shea Devon?"

"Jackie, cut it out. I'm serious here."

Jackie continued to chuckle. "I'm sorry, Shea. I just never thought I'd hear those words coming out of your mouth—a life beyond work. I have to tell you, I'm delighted to hear it. Fuck Howard if he can't deal with someone unwilling to work seven days a week, twenty-four seven. I'm glad you stood up to him."

"There's more," Shea said softly, a fist of anxiety clenching in her gut.

"Go on."

"Here's the thing. I know this assignment is the chance of a lifetime, and Howard is a great mentor for the right person, but I—I'm not willing to pay the price anymore. I thought I was ready for this change, but it turns out I bit off more than I can chew. Or more than I want to chew." She paused and then came out with it. "I want to come back. I want to come home."

She held her breath, steeling herself for the barrage of questions and the blast of incredulity. To her surprise, Jackie just said, "Shea, sweetie, if you want to come home, book the next flight out."

It took Shea a second to process what her best friend had just said. "Wait, what? Really?"

Jackie laughed, "Really. Howard will be just fine on his own for a few days or weeks, or whatever it takes to get a replacement second-in-command. Don't forget, there are two guys here in the Houston office champing at the bit to step into your shoes." Shea remained speechless, though her heart was doing back flips of joy in her chest.

"Look," Jackie continued, "you tried it and you recognized it's not for you. Kudos to you for that. Do you know how many people spend a lifetime doing something they hate, mainly because they're too scared to admit to themselves or anyone else that they made the wrong choice?"

"Yeah, I guess," Shea agreed.

"There's always a place for you here at the Houston office, you know that," Jackie continued. "If you want to know, I feel like I've lost my right arm since you've been gone. But it's more than that. Things aren't the same without my best pal around."

"Oh, Jackie, you have no idea what a weight this is off me. I was so worried about letting you down."

"Not to worry. I don't think you could if you tried. Now," Jackie said, "out with it. Who is this *friend* you were willing to risk your job for? Something tells me he's a lot more than a friend, so what's going on?" Without giving Shea a chance to respond, Jackie blurted, "Oh my god! You called Peter Roden, didn't you? See, I told you he was a good guy. You can thank me later. First, spill the beans. I want all the details."

Shea laughed. "No, Jackie. I did not call Peter Roden. This is someone else. And yes, he is a lot more than a friend. He's the most wonderful man in the world."

"Shea, that's fabulous, but when did you even have time to meet someone?"

"Remember that guy I met on the island vacation?"

"Shea, sweetie—" Jackie began in a solicitous tone.

"No," Shea interrupted. "You can stop right there, Jackie. Liam Jordan is not a fantasy. He wasn't just playing a part for that week in paradise. He's more real than anything or anyone who has ever been in my life. He flew to London to be with me, and he's even willing to relocate here, but it's not what I want. I want to be with him, but I also want to be in Houston, where our lives are. I love him, Jackie. And he loves me. For the first time in my life, I'm happy. Really happy."

She waited for Jackie's well-meaning but misplaced skepticism, but again her friend surprised her. "That's fantastic, Shea. I knew there was a warm, beating heart beneath all that drive and ambition. I'm so happy for you. I'll handle things with Howard and Dave Sutton. You just hurry up and come home."

~*~

The Houston traffic was snarled as always, and Shea's neck ached with tension from an exhausting day at the office. The phone rang on the car's Bluetooth system, announcing that Liam was on the line.

"Hi," Shea said brightly, refusing to let the stress of the day enter her voice. Since she had returned to her life in Houston, she'd managed to find the balance she was seeking—working a normal week of forty hours with Jackie's blessing, and devoting her nights and weekends to the lifestyle and the man she loved.

The sparkle of the diamond on her left ring finger still caught her eye at random times during the day, and she would marvel at how different her life was now that she'd found love. She spent most of her time at Liam's house, and they had agreed it made sense to put her condo up for sale, especially now that they'd set a date for their wedding.

"Sub girl," Liam said, those two small words garnering her complete unwavering attention. "When you get home, you will strip just inside the door and kneel with your forehead touching the floor, arms extended, ass up, until I enter the room."

"Oh," Shea said softly, the word pulled from her lips as she felt herself gliding effortlessly into that delicious place Liam called submissive headspace. "Yes, Sir." She drove the rest of the way on autopilot, the time drifting easily by.

When she stepped into the foyer, she glanced quickly around. Liam was nowhere in sight. She set her briefcase on the table by the door and stepped out of her shoes. She took off her suit jacket and skirt and folded them neatly on her briefcase. In short order she added her bra, panties and stockings.

She knelt on the hardwood floor, assuming the position as instructed, her heart beating in anticipation. She took a deep breath and let it out slowly as she waited with as much submissive patience as she could bring to bear.

It wasn't long before she heard Liam's quiet tread as he entered the foyer. She felt the light tap on her shoulder that signaled her to rise. Mustering all her grace, she lifted herself to a kneeling position, palms on her thighs, eyes downcast.

"Stand up," Liam commanded.

Shea rose to her feet. Liam took her into his arms and kissed her, his lips sending a flood of joyous light through her body. Finally he let her go. "Come," he said, leading her into the living room. He brought her to the sofa and indicated she should sit. She sank back against the cushions, her nipples tingling, her sex moistening with desire as she stared up at her handsome man.

He smiled down at her, his eyes glittering with lust and power. "You're going to use your hand to bring yourself to orgasm," he informed her as he crouched in front of her. "No matter what I do to you, your job is focus on your orgasm, so that when I tell you to come, you will come. Understood, sub girl?"

If it was possible Shea sank even deeper into submissive headspace. "Yes, Sir," she whispered. She brought her hand to her smooth, already-slick cunt and began to rub in a circle around her clit, her eyes locked on Liam's face.

He reached for her breasts, catching her nipples between his forefingers and thumbs and twisting until she gasped. "Focus," he commanded, his eyes boring into hers. The pain emanating at her nipples heightened the pleasure of her fingers at her sex and she was close to climaxing.

A sudden flick of Liam's hand across her face made Shea's hand fall away from her cunt, reaching up automatically to cradle her stinging cheek. "Liam!" she gasped in shock.

He didn't answer, except by slapping her other cheek. Shea began to pant, shock and desire crashing inside her mind like thunderclouds. He slapped her again. "Don't stop what you're doing. Spread your legs wider. Fuck yourself with your hand. Make yourself ready for my command." He took her hand, forcibly placing it between her legs.

As she began to rub herself once more, he slapped her face again. She moaned, a feral desire rising inside her so fierce that she bared her teeth like an animal and growled. Liam's eyes were locked on hers, his gaze at once loving and fierce. "Look at me," he ordered softly but firmly. "Keep your eyes on mine." Shea was panting so hard she thought she might pass out. "Slow down. Breathe," he urged gently. "This is what you need. It's where you belong."

Shea nodded, aware deep in her bones that he was right. Something about being slapped in the face was at once terrifying and thrilling in a way she couldn't articulate and barely understood. It didn't matter. She didn't have to define it. She just had to look into Liam's deep brown eyes and feel the warmth and safety of his love.

He slapped her face again and again as she kept her hand buried in the wet heat between her legs. Her cheeks were flaming, her cunt pulsing, her breath a panting rasp in her throat. "Oh god," she moaned, unable to stop the rise of pleasure that threatened to crash over her.

Liam slapped her once more. "Do it. Come for me. Now."

Her head fell back, her fingers flying as her spirit tilted on the edge of the world and then flew into space. Liam was there to catch her. Lifting himself to the sofa beside her, he took her into his arms and held her close as a powerful climax shuddered through her body.

All the exhaustion and stress she'd let take her over during the course of the work day had vanished completely. She felt revitalized, at once relaxed and invigorated, calm yet enlivened.

Shea reached for Liam, taking his face in her hands. There was so much she wanted to say, to express, to convey, to share about the joy and passion that had come into her life since she'd met this amazing man. But then, he knew it all already, didn't he? Their connection went beyond words, and had from the moment they'd laid eyes on each other.

In the end, she said the only thing that really mattered, the thing that said it all.

"I love you, Liam Jordan. With all my heart."

~*~

"It feels so good to be back. It's hard to believe it's only been six months since we met. I feel like I've known you forever." Shea and Liam were sitting on a large picnic blanket beneath a swaying palm tree on their private island in paradise.

Sylvia had made good on her promise to give Shea a free week on BDSM island, and she'd been happy to allow Liam to serve as the host, especially when she found out the two of them were engaged.

How different it was stepping from the boat this time, now that Shea's eyes and heart had been opened.

"You *have* known me forever, we just hadn't met yet," Liam replied, his eyes crinkling into a smile. "You were born for me, Shea." He reached for her, and Shea let herself be gathered into her lover's arms. Liam's kiss was sensual and lingering, as if he were doing a striptease with his lips and tongue. When he finally let her go, Shea's entire body thrummed with desire.

She watched as Liam reached into the picnic basket and took out the oblong jewelry box she hadn't realized he'd packed along with their lunch. He lifted the lid and removed her beautiful slave collar with almost ceremonial precision. The movements now second nature, Shea positioned herself on her knees, back straight, hands resting palms up on her thighs, breasts thrust proudly forward.

Following the lovely ritual they'd developed together, Liam said, "Shea, will you accept this symbol of my claim over your body, heart and soul?"

Her eyes locked on his, Shea reached for her hair, twisting it into a ponytail as she ducked her head forward to offer her neck. "Yes, Sir," she said, "I would be honored." As Liam buckled the thin strip of deep burgundy leather around her throat, a welcome, submissive peace settled softly over Shea's senses.

Sitting back, Liam said, "I'm going to spank you now. Strip and lie across my lap."

Already topless, Shea slipped off her bikini bottom. She lay over Liam's muscular thighs, her cheek resting against the beach blanket, her heart hammering, though the mantle of serenity still cloaked her senses. She thought back to that first spanking all those months ago, when she'd believed Liam was some kind of nut or madman. Even that very first time, though her mind had rebelled, her soul had somehow understood what was happening. Now she waited with eager anticipation, her ass tingling with expectation, her heart beating a steady tattoo against her ribs.

~*~

Liam massaged Shea's full, luscious ass cheeks, his cock rising like a bar of iron beneath her. He reached between her legs, his fingers probing her wet, hot cunt. When she began to squirm and sigh, he pulled his hand away, cupped his palm and brought it down against the soft, smooth skin of her perfect ass, the sound of contact cracking in the air.

Shea didn't cry out or jerk away, a small intake of breath her only reaction. Over the months she had built up a significant tolerance to erotic pain, and often asked for more. Liam had to be careful, aware of a sub's loss of perspective when in the throes of an altered state brought about by erotic pain. No matter how far he went, she always wanted more, which was just as it should be. But it was up to him to make sure he didn't give her more than she could safely handle.

He started slowly, warming the skin, acclimating the nerve endings to the onslaught of his hard, sure hand. As the spanking intensified, Shea began to curl her toes, her hands clenching into fists, her breath now a pant. "Slow your breathing, Shea," he reminded her. "Relax your body. Flow with the pain."

She took a deep, shuddering breath and let it out slowly, her fingers unfurling as she did so, her feet relaxing. He resumed the spanking, harder now, building up bit by bit, fascinated and thrilled as he always was by the reddening skin of her ass and thighs. He could actually feel the resistance leaving her body, her muscles relaxing fully against him as her lips parted and her eyes closed.

There was a blissful expression on her face, though he was hitting her quite hard now, much harder than he would have dared before she was trained. But Liam understood she was no longer processing the blows as pain. Or more accurately, the pain was taking her to a place of such infinite peace that it was worth the cost.

When Shea entered that altered state, Liam felt as if he were flying by her side, soaring over the heavens of a special sort of ecstasy. It was like handling a beautifully crafted kite caught in a powerful wind. It was up to Liam as her Dom to keep hold of the strings that kept them both tethered to the earth.

When he gauged she'd had enough, Liam began to ease the intensity of the spanking, shifting downward until he was just patting her bottom. She was limp against him, her breathing deep and even. "Hey," he whispered, leaning down and lifting the hair that had fallen over her face and tucking it behind her ear.

Shea opened her eyes slowly, staring at him as if she were still caught in a dream, which perhaps she was. Her lips curved into a sleepy smile, her eyelids fluttering closed once more. Liam stroked her back and the still-hot skin of her ass for a long time, deeply grateful this lovely, vivacious, strong woman had come into his life.

After a while she opened her eyes again and rolled from Liam's lap, stretching languorously. "Jesus," he whispered, awestruck anew with her sheer beauty. "I have to have you, Shea. Now. I have to fuck you."

As he pulled off his bathing trunks, Shea rolled over onto her hands and knees, twisting her head back to gaze at him with blazing eyes. Liam crouched behind her, probing her wet pussy with his fingers as he gripped his shaft in his other hand.

"Please, Sir," she murmured breathlessly with a shake of her head, "please take me in the ass, Sir."

Liam nodded soberly, acutely aware of the submissive grace in her request. For, though Shea had become more comfortable with her body and less inhibited about her ass during their months together, she still resisted anal sex. It was the last area in which she held herself back, keeping herself apart from him in a way that, while not overtly disobedient, kept her from the full submission he knew she longed for, and which he, too, wanted for her.

He reached into the picnic basket and removed the tube of lubricant he always kept handy. He held out the tube in Shea's direction. "Make yourself ready for me."

As Shea took the tube, Liam noticed the slight tremble in her hands, but also the determined look on her face. She unscrewed the cap and squirted a copious amount over her fingers. Reaching back, she rubbed the lubricant between her ass cheeks. Again assuming her position on hands and knees, she thrust her sexy ass toward him in clear invitation. Looking back at him, she said in a determined tone, "I want to submit fully to you. I want to withhold nothing from you."

Liam crouched again behind her, this time guiding the head of his cock between her ass cheeks. He pushed gently against her tiny hole, feeling the yield of the muscle as he slipped inside. She remained still as he carefully entered the tight passage, though he could feel the tension in her body.

"Stop resisting me, sub girl," he said, his mouth close to her ear. "Hold nothing back, as you promised."

"Yes," she said in a low, sexy voice. She pushed back against him, her tight ass grasping his cock like a close-fitting glove. Liam sighed his pleasure and began to move inside her. Balancing himself on his knees, he reached around Shea's body, his fingers seeking and finding her perfect cunt. As he thrust inside her, he massaged and teased the hard marble of her clit and the wet, swollen folds of her labia.

She began to moan, pushing back against his thrusts, her body trembling, her breasts swaying, her breathing ragged. "Yes," she cried. "Oh, god, yes! Please, yes, yes, oh, Sir, please, may I come?"

"Yes, come for me, Shea." Liam slammed into her, his fingers still buried in her pussy so that he felt the spasms of her climax as he came inside her. They tilted forward in slow motion toward the blanket and lay as they fell, Shea sprawled beneath Liam, whose heart beat like a drum against her back.

Eventually Liam summoned the strength to roll away from Shea, worried he was crushing her. Reaching for her, he pulled the beautiful, naked girl into his arms and they lay that way for a long time, letting the soft sea breeze waft over them as the waves sang a rhythmic lullaby.

The sun was setting when they finally sat up. Liam stood and held out his hand. Shea took it, allowing him to help her to her feet. They walked hand in hand toward the clear, turquoise water. It felt cool and refreshing after being outside so long in the warm sun.

When they were at waist height, Liam turned and lifted Shea into his arms. Carrying her, he moved deeper until they were past the waves, bending his knees so they floated together in the calm, peaceful waters.

He pulled her closer and turned with her toward the setting sun, which was painting the water with long lines of shimmery gold. Only when the fiery disk slipped below the horizon did Liam turn back toward the shore.

They walked together onto the cooling sand and Liam took Shea once more into his arms. "Brrr, I'm freezing," she said, wrapping her arms around her naked body. Liam reached down to pluck a towel from the blanket and wrap it around the shivering girl.

"I know just how to warm you up once we get back to the bungalow," Liam said with a broad grin and waggling eyebrows.

"I bet you do," Shea said with a laugh.

Liam gazed down at the woman who had taught him more about the power and beauty of D/s than he would have thought possible. A single, bright star appeared in the deepening sky as they moved together, dancing to the music of their shared laughter.

Available at Romance Unbound Publishing (http://romanceunbound.com)

A Lover's Call
A Princely Gift
Accidental Slave
Alternative Treatment
Binding Discoveries
Blind Faith
Cast a Lover's Spell
Caught: Punished by Her Boss
Closely Held Secrets
Club de Sade
Confessions of a Submissive
Continuum of Desire
Dare to Dominate
Dream Master
Face of Submission
Finding Chandler
Forced Submission
Frog
Golden Angel
Golden Boy
Heart of Submission
Heart Thief
Island of Temptation

Jewel Thief
Julie's Submission
Lara's Submission
Masked Submission
Obsession: Girl Abducted
Odd Man Out
Perfect Cover
Pleasure Planet
Princess
Safe in Her Arms
Sarah's Awakening
Seduction of Colette
Slave Academy
Slave Castle
Slave Gamble
Slave Girl
Slave Island
Slave Jade
Sold into Slavery
Sub for Hire
Submission in Paradise
Submission Times Two
Switch
Texas Surrender
The Abduction of Kelsey
The Auction
The Compound
The Cowboy Poet
The Master

The Solitary Knights of Pelham Bay
The Story of Owen
The Toy
Tough Boy
Tracy in Chains
True Kin Vampire Tales:
    Sacred Circle
    Outcast
    Sacred Blood
True Submission
Two Loves for Alex
Two Masters for Alexis
Wicked Hearts

Connect with Claire

Website: http://clairethompson.net
Romance Unbound Publishing:
http://romanceunbound.com
Twitter: http://twitter.com/CThompsonAuthor
Facebook:
http://www.facebook.com/ClaireThompsonauthor

Made in the USA
San Bernardino, CA
18 June 2016

DEDICATION

To anyone who ever gave me a book.

CONTENTS

A Quick Note

chapter 1	2
chapter 2	13
chapter 3	21
chapter 4	31
chapter 5	39
chapter 6	51
chapter 7	61
chapter 8	70
chapter 9	80
chapter 10	87
chapter 11	95
chapter 12	108
chapter 13	124
chapter 14	132
chapter 15	141
chapter 16	150